REBELS & RAINBOWS

An Australasian Queer Speculative Anthology

Acknowledgement of Country:

In the spirit of reconciliation, Deadset Press acknowledges the Traditional Custodians of country throughout Australia and their connections to land, sea and community. We pay our respect to their Elders past and present and extend that respect to all Aboriginal and Torres Strait Islander peoples today.

Contents

Love and Other Liminal Spaces

A.R. Henderson

The door appeared about an hour into the party, right when Addie had been thinking about going home.

"And you're sure it wasn't there before?" asked Tom, swirling a bright pink vodka mixer contemplatively in their hand.

"Of course I'm fucking sure," snapped Addie. She glared at the door and the door looked impassively back at her. There wasn't anything that weird about it. It was made of the same warm-toned brown wood as the other doors, window frames, and cabinets in Celeste's family's house, an elegant brown glass bauble serving as its doorknob. It complemented the sage green and sunset orange of the '70s style wallpaper. Dizzying geometric patterns covered a wall that had been notably door-less until five minutes earlier.

"Adelaide." Tom put on their best Teacher Voice. "Calm down, please."

Addie swung around and slugged them in the arm.

Tom yelped and crumpled sideways, spinning helplessly and miming crashing into the staircase behind them. In spite of everything, a laugh bumped up Addie's throat. Tom made a big show of pouting and looking pained, but Addie caught them smiling.

She took a deep breath, inhaling the chaotic perfume of the summer night: fruity drinks, freshwater on grass, and a whole Year Twelve cohort's worth of sweat and deodorant. She steadied herself and tried to tune out the clatter of voices from the nearby kitchen and the music wafting in from the lounge. A pop princess was crooning out a sad, synth-y song on the speakers. A stray thought pinged around Addie's head. *Is that what Celeste listens to these days? Is this her favourite music?*

She'd ask her, but Addie hadn't seen their gracious hostess since she arrived.

Addie actually hadn't seen Celeste since that day on the sports oval. It had been Addie's free period and she'd spread her laptop and study notes out in the shade of the treeline, hoping that nobody noticed she was really just messaging Tom about the latest fantasy romance novel she'd borrowed from the library. She wasn't doing her science homework, sure, but she was doing *an* experiment. Addie had picked one with a straight romance for a change and was seeking Tom's expertise, as someone attracted to men, whether he agreed that the male love interest was an annoying dirtbag. Tom had mostly been sending green-faced vomiting emojis in response to Addie's plot recap, which seemed conclusive.

Addie was in the middle of summarising a particularly ridiculous scene, chewing on a grin as she typed, when Celeste said "Hi!" Addie flinched so hard she nearly threw her phone onto the field.

She hadn't heard anyone approach; she half-wondered if she'd imagined the girl's voice, an echo from a memory. Yet when she looked up, dazed, there she was. Celeste, with her grey P.E. t-shirt clinging to her, sweat shimmering like sunlight on water in the delicate dips of her collarbones. Celeste, catching the brightness and warmth of the November afternoon like a stained-glass window. Celeste, affecting the gravity around Addie and causing her stomach to swoop as if the ground had gone out from underneath her—a feeling always followed by a spark of flinty rage, which in turn always dulled to a nostalgic ache.

Celeste had smiled a straight-toothed and gloss-lipped smile straight at Addie, and, for some godforsaken reason, invited her to the party she was hosting that Saturday. "It would be nice to see you there," she'd said. And then, like the afterimage of a dream, like the morning dew in the rising sun, the little shit was *gone*, jogging away to rejoin her P.E. class.

Addie convinced herself it wasn't a big deal. *Everyone* was invited to the party—it was Celeste's philanthropic gift to the year group, offered alongside glittering bittersweet tears and some guff about how *we're all going our separate ways soon.* Well, that was true for *her.* Addie had overheard some of the other stage crew guys talking about how Celeste had gotten into some fancy-pants Melbourne university, but was taking a gap year first and going on a tour of Europe.

Addie would have loved to ask Celeste if that was true. She would also have loved to ask her about the fucking door.

"Well where does it go?" Tom pulled themself out of their dramatic fall, smoothing down the front of their souvenir *Hadestown* t-shirt.

"I don't know," replied Addie, and it tasted like half a lie. Tom squinted at her, then reached for the doorknob. Addie flinched forward to stop them, an electric reflex. Another reflex sent her craning her neck to see what was inside.

They twisted the handle and pulled the door open, revealing a dimly-lit hallway papered with the same hypnotising green-and-orange wallpaper and floored with dark wooden slats. It stretched like a throat into the house, vanishing into darkness at the end where it gave way to a set of descending stairs. An incandescent mix of fear, rage, and joy flared in Addie's chest.

Tom shut the door, shoulders peaking. Addie watched as they opened the door again, peeking inside to see the same hallway and staircase. Tom snapped the door closed a second time, made a bee-like humming sound, then turned on their heel and sped down the hall.

Addie followed as Tom walked around the nearest corner and into the kitchen—the room on the other side of the psychedelic wall. The ochre-tiled room was crammed with students laughing, drinking, and in the middle of their own in-depth conversations, a couple making out against the sink.

Tom looked at the fridge and cabinets stacked against the wall. Then back into the corridor, directly on the other side of said wall, and at the door that opened into an impossible space.

"Yeah nah," they announced. "That's fucked."

Addie breathed out. "It's exactly how I remember it."

#

She had been in Year Six—at the top of the cresting wave of youth before being dumped onto the sandbar of high school. In the memory, Celeste and Addie were in that same kitchen. Celeste poured out a bowl of salt and vinegar chips and asked Addie, "Do you think that new boy Chris is cute?"

Addie, mesmerised by the way Celeste's hair turned the colour of honey in the sunshine streaming in through the window, lied and said "Yeah, he's hot."

Celeste's pretty face pinched, then smoothed out into a smile. Chips in hand, she headed out into the corridor and towards the staircase that would ferry them both up to Celeste's bedroom.

Across from the stairs was a door, standing in the middle of the trippy green-and-orange wall. Celeste stopped, and Addie pulled up short behind her. "What is it?"

Celeste looked at the door, hugging the chip bowl to her chest. Addie knew all the quirks and crinkles of her face—they were best friends, after all—but her expression, then, was hard to read. She turned and smiled at Addie, a much more natural and glowing one than the grin from the kitchen. "Do you want to see something cool?"

Addie would have followed Celeste to the moon, so she thought nothing of following Celeste through the door and along a softly-lit hallway, then down the flight of wooden stairs that came after it. It hadn't occurred to Addie to question the physics of it at the time. She was too busy watching Celeste's back, the way her ponytail bounced as she skipped down the stairs, the way her voice rose and fell like music. "I come down here sometimes when I want to think."

The stairs took them down into a brick-walled basement, the kind Addie had only seen in American movies. A fluffy cream-coloured rug took up most of the floor, and on top of it was a squishy-looking couch upholstered in a bright sky blue rather than the earthy tones of Celeste's parents' mid-century furniture. Addie stared around the basement, taking in the posters on the walls and the bookshelf crammed with magazines and paperbacks. The room was windowless and the only light came from a frilly table lamp set on top of the shelf, which Addie could have sworn switched itself on when they arrived at the bottom of the stairs.

"This rules!" cried Addie. "You have this all to yourself?"

"Yep! It's my special place." Celeste flung herself onto the cushions and giggled.

"Am I allowed in here?"

Celeste opened her mouth in a horrified O shape. "Of course you are! What do you think this is?" And she thrust out her wrist and pointed to the beaded friendship bracelet strapped there. Addie let herself grin, let herself giggle, and launched herself onto the couch to join Celeste. Two girls with matching purple-and-white beads on their arms and a secret room and a bowl of chippies to themselves.

Addie had no idea how much time passed, but the two of them emerged to find their respective mothers chatting over the kitchen countertops. "Now where have you been?" Addie's mum made a big show of looking at her watch.

Addie grinned. "The basement! It's so cool down there! Mum, how come Celeste gets a whole underground room to hang out in but I still have to share a room with Rachel?"

The adults, collectively, blinked. Beside Addie, Celeste seized up. The slightest bit. A fraction of a shift in her posture.

"What do you mean by that?" Celeste's mother frowned in a way that sharpened all her features.

Addie opened her mouth to explain. "It's re—"

Celeste cut her off. "She's kidding."

Addie whipped around to stare at Celeste. She tittered out a crystalline little laugh, not meeting Addie's eye. "We were making up plans for our ideal future house," Celeste told them. "I said we could live in a house with a basement games room."

"We were there for ages!" Addie protested, filled with hot fumes. "It's the room down the stairs!" She ran out of the kitchen and around the corner, down the walkway sandwiched between the staircase and that awful hypnotic wallpaper.

And found herself facing an empty wall. No door. Just a couple of family photos. Her stomach dropped through the floor.

"Adelaide, we don't have a basement." Celeste's mother gave her a vulturish look as Addie ran her hands over the wall. Addie's mother apologised. Addie stared helplessly at Celeste and Celeste said absolutely nothing.

#

When she felt like lying to herself, Addie thought that she and Celeste would have drifted apart anyway. High school happened. Childhood friendships didn't always stick. They veered towards different social groups and different hobbies. Addie cut her hair short and started drawing weird art and clumsily kissing girls, Celeste started wearing makeup and taking pristine selfies with boys. Addie watched from the fringes as Celeste shone in the spotlight, one of those magical beings who was somehow liked by everyone. Except Addie, the one person who had a BFF bracelet stashed in the bottom of a drawer somewhere. She'd thrown it out, once, but then retrieved it from the bin ten minutes later.

Celeste had been so certain and so convincing when she said *she's kidding* that day. Maybe Addie *had* imagined the basement, or remembered that afternoon wrong.

Fuck that. Addie knew it had been real. She didn't know how, but she knew. She also knew that Celeste had been happy to belittle her, to pass her off as a liar, a silly child playing pretend. It hadn't been *oops, we made a mistake!* It had been *Addie was kidding.*

If she'd wanted to keep the door a secret, she could've just told me. Addie wondered if Celeste had even wanted to share the hidden room with her that day. If Celeste wanted her around at all. She had been so, so quick to throw Addie under the bus while she remained, poised, on the side of the road.

An impossible door had appeared in the wall and broken Addie's foolish little heart. And now, six years later, she was standing in front of it again.

#

"You're not going *in?*" Tom's eyes whizzed back and forth between Addie and the yawning neck of the hallway.

Addie wiped her palms on her tattered denim shorts. "I need to see if that basement's still there."

"You can't just wander into random rooms in someone else's house. Especially if they're laws-of-physics-defying liminal spaces that aren't always there."

"Why would the hallway appear if it didn't want me to go into it?"

She stepped across the threshold as Tom spluttered "Way to victim-blame the door! I mean. . . what? Addie, seriously, don't."

Her boots clapped against the dark wooden slats. Even a few steps in, the hallway dampened the sound of the party, as if the hubbub in the kitchen was happening down the street instead of in the next room. Everything faded to a pillowy echo except for the sound of Addie's own breathing and the distant rattle of Tom protesting from the doorway. She kept walking, heading for the top of the stairs. The stairs that would lead her to Celeste's basement and prove it had all been real.

"I'll be back in one sec, okay?" she called. Behind her, Tom did not reply.

Addie alighted on the top step. It wasn't well-lit, and it was difficult to see the bottom of the staircase, so she took it careful but fast. One stair, then another, steam-powered by the anger that had made a home in her chest that day and had smouldered for the entirety of high school.

Addie allowed herself to picture the undignified shock on Celeste's face when she yelled at her about this. *I fucking told you this house had a basement,* she'd say. Picture-perfect Celeste, top of the class, fit and pretty, generous enough to invite *everyone* to her parents' stylish house. Well, it was an illusion—the house had a weird secret staircase in it, and therefore Celeste couldn't be perfect, either. Addie allowed herself a snicker at the mental image of Celeste's glossy smile trembling, ready to crumble.

Addie caught her breath. This was strangely tiring. And shouldn't she be at the bottom by now?

In front of her, the stairs continued: three steps before the darkness ate them. She frowned and slowly turned to look over her shoulder. Above her, the staircase extended until the top of it blurred and vanished into the distant glow of the hallway lights.

Her stomach climbed into her throat. She tried to swallow it down.

"Tom?" Her voice echoed against the stairwell walls—wallpapered in absurd patterns of green and orange—reverberating back against her but going nowhere. No reply came from above.

"Well," Addie grumbled into the dark. "Shitballs."

When she had been here last, the trip downstairs had been exciting because she'd been following Celeste. Alone, it occurred to her how claustrophobic the space was. The geometric shapes on the wall seemed to wriggle.

Addie stuck out her jaw and stomped down the stairs.

One, two, three, four steps. "You can't go forever," she told the staircase. "The basement has to be around here somewhere."

As if in reply, a landing appeared three steps down: a little offshoot from the main stairs that led to another door. Addie frowned, then opened it, a matching glass doorknob under her sweaty palm. On the other side was another hallway, leading to another staircase—this one going up.

The hall was identical save for the direction of the stairs, and a flash of pastel blue amidst the dark browns, greens, and oranges: a heap of fabric chucked over the banister. Addie reached for it and pinched what turned out to be a sleeve. Someone had left their flouncy little cardigan. "Is there someone else in here?" she called, not sure who she was asking. When she turned around to go back the way she'd come, the door to the landing was gone.

"Oh, fuck off with that," muttered Addie. She sucked in a lungful of stale, woodsy-smelling air and started up the new staircase. Something in the space creaked. She whipped around, but there was nothing there, just stairs, and stairs, and stairs. She told herself it was just her weight on old wood.

Fourteen steps later, another landing, another door. Beyond that, another hallway. Was Addie imagining it, or had the patterns on the wallpaper changed, getting bigger and flashier, their greens and oranges brighter? Or were her eyes just adjusting to the odd, stale darkness?

She checked her phone and, of course, it had no bloody signal. Another creak echoed from somewhere behind her and she spun around, heart hammering at her sternum as if it wanted to get out of her ribs as much as Addie wanted to get out of the hallways.

"Tom!" she threw dignity to the wind and ran, lungs burning. *Tom!*

Another door, another hallway. Addie forced herself not to cry. She had never been a crier, it was too vulnerable and wet. She yelled instead, shouting out the fire in her chest. "Let me out, you fuckhouse!" She stormed to the end of the hall and kicked the next door open. *"To-o-o-om!"*

Another set of stairs. Addie ran up them, two at a time. "Tom!"

Six stairs up, she wasn't sure what possessed her, but instead she tried yelling *"Celeste!"*

She flung open the next door and spilled out into the corridor outside the kitchen.

Her momentum flung her straight into Tom's chest, colliding with the red carnation flower printed on their *Hadestown* shirt with enough force to flatten her nose. Noise, noise, *noise* rushed back to her, the hitch and rush of chatting voices, the clink of glassware, the screech of cicadas outside.

"Addie, you scared the *shit* out of me!" Tom's voice cut through the clamour. They grabbed her shoulders and she lolled back her head to see their face, shocked to see the fear there. Not the over-the-top stage-acting fear that she'd seen in school productions, but the bloodshot eyes of real terror.

She forced her breathing to steady. The speakers in the lounge were now playing a rap song, one she'd heard over and over again on the radio at the café where she worked on weekends. Was any of this Celeste's actual taste in music, she wondered in a daze, or was she just playing the most popular hits? The widest appeal, the lowest common denominator—the party playlist of a chronic people-pleaser?

Addie made herself focus. "How long was I in there?"

"Like, twenty minutes! And you didn't answer my texts *and* didn't respond when I called you. I panicked and went to look for Celeste, but I don't know where the fuck she is! At her *own* party! Fuck!" Tom spun away, hands in their hair.

"Are you done?"

"Fuck!" Tom cleared their throat. "Yes. Now I'm done. What happened to you? Did you find the basement?"

Addie leaned on her knees. "Um. No. It's a little different to what I remember."

She glanced over her shoulder. The door was still there. She gave it the finger.

#

Addie got a big glass of water, because somehow it seemed like the sensible thing to do after nearly getting eaten by a fuckarse labyrinth of non-Euclidean hallways.

She sat, sipping, on the hallway floor, facing the door and making sure it didn't go anywhere. Under the chirpy pop-rock track playing on the living room speakers, Addie overheard Tom ask two of their nearby classmates if anyone had seen Celeste.

"I'm surprised she's got time to host a party at all," said one. "Didn't she get into law school in Sydney? She's probably pre-studying."

The other blew a cloud of strawberry-scented vapour. "Nah, she got picked up for some modelling contract, didn't she? Someone scouted her from Instagram and she's moving to New York, or something."

"It might be both," their friend shrugged. "Remember how she managed that whole charity festival thingy last year even though it crossed over with exam period? I wish I could multitask like that."

"You're both useless, thank you," said Tom. "And don't smoke in the house."

Yeah, thought Addie. *The house won't like it.*

She shivered, despite how sweaty she was in the hot night. In front of her, the door hung ajar, like an open mouth. Maybe like an extended hand.

Tom returned, rolling their eyes. "Quick survey says no one has seen Celeste all night. Which sounds like a recipe for disaster even without the whole endless hallway situation, but. . ."

"Tom," Addie stood up. "I need to go back in."

They stared at her for a long, long moment, long enough for the song playing in the lounge to change. Country music twanged in the backdrop as they picked up their vodka mixer from where they'd put it down on the stairs. Addie went to speak and Tom held up a single, silencing finger as they swallowed the last of the bright pink liquid.

"Okay." They rolled their shoulders, looked at the ceiling, did a couple of vocal warm-ups, then met Addie's eye. "Okay. But I'm not just tossing you into the hole. Have we got like. . . a rope?"

Addie crossed her arms, cocking an eyebrow. "No, sorry, I left my bondage gear in the car. What do you *mean*, have we got a rope?"

"I mean to tie around your waist so I can pull you back out, or something!" Tom swatted at her. "Don't act like you've never heard of that before!"

"There might be a leash around here somewhere. One of those extendable ones." She stuck a finger through one of the belt loops on her jean shorts. "Celeste has a dog."

"Ooh, pretty sure she doesn't," Tom grimaced. "Celeste posted a memorial for a Cocker Spaniel on her socials like, two months ago."

Pickles died? Acid spiked through Addie's gut—the strange in-between grief for the pet of someone she used to know. She tried to surge past it. "Okay, well, they probably still have the leash. Right?"

Tom shook their head, fingertips against their temples. "That's going to be what, two metres long? It won't be enough."

"Alright, so. . . some other way of marking where I've already been so I don't get lost?"

Tom lowered their hands and clapped them together. "Go full Hansel and Gretel mode."

"We don't have breadcrumbs, but. . ." she glanced towards the kitchen, struck by the memory of twelve-year-old Celeste pouring a packet of chips into a bowl.

She and Tom snuck into the kitchen to find the crowd thinning out, reduced to a (different) couple kissing against the countertop and some goth-looking kids having a serious philosophical debate over the pizza boxes. Tucked on the bench by the fridge were several half-full bags of potato chips, pretzels, and mixed nuts.

"We'll use salt and vinegar," declared Tom, plucking the bag by its corner as if reluctant to touch too much of it at once. "No one will mind."

"What have salt and vinegar chips ever done to you?"

"Uh, destroyed the inside of my mouth with extreme and deliberate violence?" They stuck out their tongue and tossed her the packet. "These are *nobody's* favourite flavour."

Addie caught the bag and cupped it against her chest, breathing in their intense fragrance. Something so sour shouldn't have made her nostalgic.

She and Tom faced the door and its impossible hallway. "You're sure about this?"

"Stop asking me that. I'll freak out."

"Shut up. Asking *are you okay?* is what you do when you care about someone." They squeezed her shoulder. "Okay, go before you freak out. As the priestess says, *good luck, babe.*"

Bag of chips in hand, Addie walked in.

#

"Sorry for littering," she said, setting down a salt and vinegar chip on the hallway floor. She left another one on the top step of the dark staircase, then began her descent. The house did not reply—was she expecting it to?—just stretched ahead of her. One, two, three, four, five steps into the soupy dimness, swallowing her down a colourful, patterned throat. Addie watched her feet and just walked, setting a chip down every five steps. Except. . . wait, had that been five, or six? She swore under her breath, then forced herself to inhale through her teeth. "Sorry for yelling, too. Before, I mean. I went the wrong way and flipped shit."

It had been about this time that the landing had appeared, before. Addie kept descending the stairs and tried not to think too hard about if that meant anything. "This was way more straightforward when I was a kid," she told the house. "But I guess most things have gotten more complicated since then."

Addie wondered if things had ever been *simple* between her and Celeste— for as long as she could remember, her feelings for Celeste been crammed clumsily in the middle of the Venn diagram between love, friendship, and hate, one emotion never quite able to cancel out the other. Were they *just old friends?* Were they enemies? Did they even matter to each other anymore? What was the best name for the adoring resentment that Addie had worn like an elastic friendship bracelet, squeezing so hard it left a mark, for the past six years?

She had told herself a hundred million times to let the girl go. Addie had found new friends, learning to do set design and tech support for the drama kids, swapping stupid memes about Broadway shows and fantasy novels, spiralling into complex conversations about attraction and gender identity and queer complications no one else would *get*. Addie had found a new best friend in Tom, fitting together like a pair of wrongly-cut puzzle pieces that nonetheless matched. Addie had all that, and Celeste. . .

It occurred to her that whenever she looked over at Celeste, the girl had been alone. Always surrounded by people, always smiling, always sparkling, but always standing out like a figurehead. A doll on a shelf. A pretty poster in a solo frame. The hostess of a party where everyone was having a great time without any idea where she was.

Addie realised she had stopped counting the steps. She was trying to think if she'd ever seen Celeste lost in raucous laughter at nonsense in-jokes, lying in a pile of friends. If she'd ever seen Celeste looking moony-eyed and sincere at any of the pretty boys she briefly dated. Did she even really like them? Or was that a performance too, something she felt like she had to do to save face and keep it normal, like denying the existence of the basement?

Surely not, right? Celeste could have heaps going on that Addie wasn't privy to. Surely she had someone else to share her personal highs and lows with? Surely she had *someone* who she opened up to?

"Shit." Addie stopped short. She'd nearly run into a door.

The house was quiet, all sounds of music and chatter reduced to a faraway heartbeat. Addie's breath was loud in the dim space. She shifted the bag of chips from one hand to the other and reached for the doorknob, preparing to dive into the heart of the maze.

The door opened into the basement.

The monster at the heart of the labyrinth was curled up on the sky blue couch, wearing a white sundress and a streaky pink face. Celeste flinched, startled, and stared at Addie in bloodshot confusion. That honey-coloured hair was stuck to her forehead in stringy tendrils and a bubble of snot was hanging out her button nose. Addie took a small, petty moment to appreciate that Celeste looked like shit.

Celeste, perfect and pristine Celese—overachiever, sporting star, friends with everyone and spending a party alone in a basement that shouldn't exist. Addie took in the girl in front of her, the person for whom she'd harboured a crush and a grudge for so many years, love and resentment smouldering alongside each other. Maybe they would all go their separate ways after tonight, after graduation. But Addie had a feeling Celeste wouldn't be too far away. *You never forget your first love, or something*, she thought. You never forget the girl who led you down a flight of impossible stairs to a space that couldn't be real.

Addie said, gently, "I told you this house had a fucking basement."

"Addie?" Celese blinked like a startled cartoon deer, then wiped her eyes with the heels of her hands. "The. . . that's. . . what are you doing here?"

"You invited me, remember? Said it would be good to see each other." Addie couldn't help but smile as her old friend attempted damage control, tried to stitch her flawless façade back together. Addie held out the bag of salt and vinegar crisps. "Chippy?"

Celeste blinked at her again, almost warily, then croaked "Sure, thanks."

Addie crossed the room and sat on the blue couch. It was the same one from back then—most of the furniture was familiar, though there were some new additions to the bookshelf. *She still comes here when she wants to be alone,* Addie mused. *And when she wants to enjoy smutty fantasy novels where no-one can catch her. Hey, I've read that one. . .*

"How is it up there?" Celeste's voice was wet. "Oh, I shouldn't be—is everything okay? Is everyone having a good time?"

Addie frowned. Celeste sniffled, then wiped her eyes again. Addie resisted the urge to reach out and grab her dainty little wrists, hold them still, force Celeste to let herself cry. "It's fine. Are *you* okay?"

"I'm good." Celeste's voice hitched up, almost musically, before her sweet, weepy visage crumpled into a scowl. "I'm just feeling, um, a little overwhelmed."

Must be all those fancy universities you got into. Addie considered teasing her about the rumours of her excellence, but the words fizzled out on her tongue. The burning in her chest had dampened, water thrown on the coals. Instead, she shrugged and said, "Fair enough."

Celese smiled a watery smile, and a silent weight melted away within Addie. She had been so ready to be angry with Celeste, now she just felt sorry for her. More than that. . . well, now she felt like she was looking at a human.

Up close, she didn't shine so brightly. Or was that just nostalgia for the last time Addie had been in this room? Was that feeling what Celeste was chasing when she sequestered herself away down here?

Do you miss me like I miss you? Addie bit her tongue before she could ask. That was a complicated question to throw at someone in such a liminal time and space.

Plus. . . well, the door had opened for Addie, hadn't it? Maybe she already had the answer.

She tried not to blush as Celeste reached over and took a chip from the bag in her hands. "Ooh, salt and vinegar."

"You think I don't remember your favourite?" asked Addie, before she could stop herself. Celeste smiled again, hiccupping out a laugh.

Celeste hunched her shoulders and nibbled a chip. Then she gave up and crammed a handful into her mouth.

Addie grinned at the sheer feral relief on her face. "When was the last time you ate something?"

"I was prepping the house all afternoon. . ." Celeste waggled her fingers as if counting hours on her hand. She had a crumb stuck to the corner of her mouth, and Addie had a magnetic impulse to wipe it off with her thumb. She quelled that, for now, but thought of something better. She stood, leaving Celeste blinking up at her.

"Come with me."

Celeste made a shocked little *hm?* noise.

Addie held out her hand, palm up. "I mean, you can stay down here if you want. But you could also come up the stairs—hopefully not too many of them, and going in normal directions—and hang out with me and Tom. Get them on a tangent about the cursed production history of *Carrie: The Musical* and you won't have to think about uni or anything for like, at *least* twenty minutes. We can put bug spray on and sit out in the garden where it's quiet, and I can nick some pizza from the kitchen."

Celeste, sitting in the middle of her maze of halls and staircases, pressed her lips together and contemplated this. Addie watched a thousand *what if*s and *but I should*s swirl through her big, wounded, stupidly gorgeous eyes.

"It's just for tonight," Addie suggested. After this everyone was going their separate ways, down whatever twisting corridors adult life might take them.

When Celeste took Addie's offered hand, they only had to walk up a single staircase and down a straight hallway. The door loomed, ajar, in front of them, leading back into the noise and clutter of the house. Celeste's palm was clammy against Addie's. Addie wasn't sure whether to be elated at the touch, or grossed out by the sweat, or whimsical about how they used to hold hands all the time as kids.

Never mind endless stairs and looping halls, Addie never felt more lost than when she was near Celeste.

They walked out through the door together. When Celeste shut it behind her, the warm-toned brown wood disappeared into the wallpaper.

ABOUT THE AUTHOR

A.R. Henderson is a writer, editor, and researcher working on Ngunnawal country. They completed a PhD in Creative Writing at the University of Canberra, where they studied LGBTQIA+ representation in young adult literature (they like to tell people that their sense of binary gender fell clean off in the middle of this project). Their short stories have appeared in literary magazines such as *Long Trek* and *#EnbyLife* and anthologies including the Aurealis Award finalist *An Unexpected Party* (Fremantle Press, 2023). You can find all their work in a nice, neat pile at arhendersonwrites.com

Memories of the Old Sun

Eugen Bacon

Sometimes you wish you were a biorobot. Unemotive, just 1s and 0s.

Your mother's words burn inside your mind: "People are laughing, others pitying. Mazu. Who'll wait on me?"

"I'm here, Mae."

"The journey is far over the seas from Konakri. Come visit before I die."

"I'll visit. I promise. And you're not dying."

"Stop giving me regret. When will you find a woman?"

"If you keep asking, I'll stop calling."

"*Aiii*, his truth comes out. He'll stop ringing."

"Are you telling the phone?"

"Who birthed you? I broke my back to raise you. Now you will kill me with regret."

"It's not like that, Mae."

"The girls here are budding. I'll negotiate a wife with a good stomach. It shows in the clan—the ones who can make babies."

"Stop it. Please."

"I know to pick the right girl. Breasts like papayas. Buttocks bigger than a pot."

"There's more to life than marriage."

An email from Jordan. In it, the photo of a marigold-eyed kitten, head cocked at the camera. You want to tell Mae about Jordan, but on a spell like today she's no listener.

You snatch yourself back to her lamenting. "Don't put me in mourning. Child, you're cutting me."

"Now you exagger—"

"There's the question of dowry."

"Is this what it's about, Mae? I'll send money."

"Of course I need money. The cows are sick. And the village's still growing—we need a well to water our yams. I told the pastor at the school—"

"The one I raised money for?"

"That one. I told the pastor I'd ask about the well."

"Being here doesn't mean I'm rolling in money."

"Now you think you're a big shot. That you can stop helping."

You sigh. Sending money home is a bottomless cup. The village, through your mother, makes it an inescapable yoke. She finally agrees to hang up, because you invent that it's midnight.

"It's night there," she says in wonderment. "Like here?"

"Yes, Mae." Your pretend yawn is loud. "And if I don't sleep, who'll make money for us tomorrow? Sooo tired."

"You take my advice—I don't want to suckle the whole village. Give me a grandchild."

"I hear you, Mae."

"By the gods, you'd better. *Mffyuu.*" She sucks her teeth, letting you know she's not letting it go.

#

Jazz knows sie's a variable. Sie has an inbuilt scrapbook filled with memories, sometimes rushing, often rusting. They twirl inside hir head. File cards full of deserts and hungriness clipped away from hir heart. They are from names in a grammar sie doesn't remember, childhood friends or secrets: Bug, Dyn, Cyclone, Bash, Allon, Prim, Krema. . .

#

MEMORIES OF THE OLD SUN

Making a biorobot is genesis—not a six-day creation, rest on the seventh, but rather a Darwinian evolution, natural selection and all. You put each zygote under lights, spin it slowly to nurture its earliest developmental stage—the unique genome sequence of human and artificial intelligence. The right genetic signature is necessary to form memories derived from mainframes and natural evolution.

Malware botches some of the zygotes and they begin to show excessive individual thought, traces of zeitgeist. You vaporize most anomalies, rain them back into the network as gametes. It doesn't matter if they had a name—all zygotes have a name—you deal with anomalies and rename them. Hundreds of zygotes each in a simulated placenta inside pods. Newborn. But only the fittest shall live.

A biorobotics engineer wants no variants, for obvious reasons. Variants generate runaway events. They display ego amplitudes, heroism complexes and random hierarchies that are circular, never linear. Inevitably, and *it is* inevitable, they fall into abeyance, putting the system into chaos.

The system demands everything exists in one voice: muted and responding only to command. Clumsy ones hit the bin, disconnected before they break synchrony. Daily, the eyes of cameras shift in a sense of rhythm and whirr, a silent opera taking down each face that might embrace self-actualization outside the greater good.

Rebooting, tagging and personal monitoring fixes the flaws of milder anomalies. Interface deconstruction tears down alpha anomalies. Intervention nullifies discord, keeping the systems in a unity of purpose. It ensures no counterpoint, convolution or polyphony: just algorithms and intelligence.

You assign each newborn to a research station that you closely monitor across the first year of extrauterine development. Then they graduate to space research stations.

\#

Sie remembers days of life and death when fate snatched sie away and sealed hir sorrow to an exact point. Days that were mistrials drowned in desire, studded with intersections where babies cried in syntax, never in melody, and lights pulsed but never turned red.

\#

That phone chat with your mother. . . you hold your head in your hands. You feel like a sea putting on tides in the dark, draping whole cities, washing away last night's news and your mother's insistence.

"My blood and sweat under the old sun put you to school—see where you are now."

"And I'm grateful, Mae."

"When your father died, you became the head of the house. Don't you forget, son."

"I won't."

A new item on the taskbar. You click the email open. Another Jordan animated gif: 'Happy Lunch Hour!' It's shaped in old gold on a beach speckled with palm trees. He fills you with good vibes.

\#

Memory is snow—iced crystals falling in clusters from the sky. Pellets big as fists, opaque yet trustless. Emotions are surface, doorsteps of a moment.

\#

There was a time when conversation with your mother was easy. But on the phone it's crumbs and shapes, what's left of language and duty. If your mother were on social media, you'd take your chances on texting. IDK, BRB, G2G. You'd get away with saying TTYL, promising to talk later, and not doing it. Maybe she'd get the idea with YGTI.

You chuckle softly, but it's only with imagining her texting you back: *WTF? YOLO. Give grandchild. ASAP.* Indeed, one only lives once. You've never been much of a swimmer yet dive into the ocean on your small screen, away from a weight of responsibility. Tradition is a beast. Why must you marry? Marriage is antiquity. There's no alchemy for a perfect one. What you remember of your parents is absence. Your father was always away. Mostly for work, sometimes with other women. You remember the fighting like thunder—you trembling under a bed as Mae and your father crashed, wrestling around the house, breaking things. You don't want to be that.

You're unhappy, but Jordan's meme that's an animated gif of huggy cartoony figures in metallic hues and pearly textures, jellybean shaped, is lifting.

#

At nights sie wakes up from pixelated cyclones in hir dreams, shapeless footsteps to hir world of amorphous vapours. Hir life is a cradle—forming, morphing hir newborn self until sie toddles out of it. Hir heart is a blizzard—the data it holds veers from science, erodes trust. It's a heart that touches petals with fists, unclear where on a flower to caress. If sie could levitate, sie'd give hirself to all the books in the universe, speak their tongues. Sie'd teach hirself magic from a book, pull out ebony rabbits and gilded coins that look easy on satellite.

#

Your eyes turn back to the job. 24/7 on live feed and reruns, no popcorn. A silver and black grid of the universe. A switch on the control splashes colour if you wished it. You watch the biorobots in their tasks across the globe. Inbuilt to take temperature, pressure, rain and wind readings. They're humanlike, no different from people on the streets. A little sentient, yet designed to be windvanes, barometers, wet and dry bulbs through human skin. They're imprinted with aerial surveillance and radius maps, motion imagery and billions of pixels in resolution splashed on your screen.

You created them. Still, sometimes you pity them. Isolated in research stations across the globe. You have four primes: Jazz, Krema, Cyclone and Bash. First-year wards in the biorobotic flock. Jazz is in Antarctica—sie was always different but you gave hir a chance from deconstruction. You remember how sie was always clingy, wanting a song, a cuddle or whatnot reassurance to perform hir best. The others don't worry you: Krema in Pelican Point, Namibia—sand-dune-filled, blazing hot oasis, miles of desert. Cyclone in Mawsynram, East India—as wet as it comes on the East Khasi Hills district. Bash in Death Valley, Eastern California—it's a furnace creek there. The government calls it Nextgen 4.0, but is it a future that you want? Each biorobot is a humanesque quantum machine.

Still, you worry about Jazz.

Jordan sends you a video funny of a big-bottomed man in blood-red dungarees dancing 'Jingle Bells' to an afro beat called ndombolo.

#

Sie remembers a world awash with sound. It feels years away, but sie remembers it. Sometimes whoosh. . . whoosh, or thump. . . thump. . . Always lub dub lub dub. Now and then a voice, hushed. Every now and then a whirr or a buzz, a hum or a drone. Sometimes beep, beep. Sie remembers jumping at a touch from outside the membrane. A gentle rub, and a song. Sie neared. Pressed hir ear to feel, to listen to the world. Hir world now. Entering it was calm in a squeeze, and then cold, then rub, more rub. And then warm full of soft. Rhythm. Melody. A fuzzy that never lasts. Hir poetry of yearning.

\#

Another Jordan funny on your phone screen is dappled with heart shapes and ruby roses.

You crave sunshine. You long for the sun back home in Konakri. You step away from the monitors, go out the door. But outside is no sun. It's full-blown winter, people in coats walking away from you on the streets. Cyclists in spandex jingle bells at drivers and shenanigans of life in the slow lane.

You smoke the city, packs of it a day. Not real darts. You stand outside the burnt-brick monolith of your workplace, same time each mid-morn, puffing the world. A few times to get going, until you feel cafés, libraries, theatres, high rises, post-offices, even ICUs—too many of them—on your tongue. You let the traffic jams and politicians linger in your mouth, telecom poles, museums, thugs, buskers, beggars, nurses, teachers wafting in too. You cast your mind on the taste of the metropolis to its last despondence, discontent, fear, fury and all. But sometimes there's awe, serenity and hope. You draw the last bit into your mouth.

At first, when you started the smoke—Jordan introduced you to it, smoking the city, as he called it—you felt dizzy, nauseous. Jordan held you as you gagged. But over time the sensation of motion sickness morphed into something complex. What you feel now is alertness. You feel real. Relaxed, away from family pressure. You feel a pleasure of yearning, a nostalgia of curiosity. But you never want anyone other than Jordan to see you like this.

Yebe! Hey you! Found a woman yet? Your mother in your head disturbs the peace of the moment. You return inside to monitor the research stations.

Your phone vibrates. It's Jordan.

"Hiya," he says.

'Hello you. How's the writing going?"

"Going," he says. "You know how it is. What's happening there?"

You want to talk about your mother, but don't. Instead, you tell him about your dream. "I was a goddess looking for new suns. Not one sun, a whiteness that's all colours of the rainbow. I was searching for many suns. Different colours."

"Right."

"I was sick of same old. What I needed was blue. A teal sun, or a chocolate cherry one. I got close to my quest but shifted into a bird. It was a bird that kept morphing. First, I was a hyacinth macaw, cobalt blue feathered. Then I was a quetzal—scarlet, indigo and olive green with a white underside on my tail."

"I'd love to see your underside tail," says Jordan.

"And then I was a red-crested turaco. Green bodied, white-faced. Running on the ground, not flying in the skies, but in sonic speed. I was screeching and jabbering, whooping out my search for the suns. It's a prophecy, do you think?"

"More like, they say dreams tell us something about ourselves."

You look at the monitors.

#

Sie remembers Daddy.

#

You made the biorobots feel safe in an engineered womb, birthed them and threw them into experiments. You trained and tested each biorobot for endurance. You shoved them into water and studied their comfort, breathing, how they positioned for buoyancy. You stuffed them in saunas and monitored their need for water, which ones—like Jazz—lost their cool. You threw them into labs swollen with sandstorms, and observed their natural compass, which ones stayed hungry yet measured. You cut off their oxygen, nearly crushed them with pressure. You studied their navigation, patience, inventiveness.

But you don't want them speculating why penguins make a beeline down a sandy hill. That's the ilk of sentience you tried rebooting out of Jazz. Sie reminds you of a bee.

#

Memory is a billion miles folded in a box. It's tucked inside a key at zero degrees staring long and hard at a wish for a bee. Because a bee prefers a garden or an orchard, a meadow or a copse—everywhere sie wants to be. Because a bee likes dandelions and black-eyed susans, and the bittersweet breath of a bouquet is better than decay. Because a bee is dusky and blond, burgundy and silver, auburn and lime, azure, even lilac: none of those hues in this dull world and its swirl of winds. Because a bee makes honey, and it is thick and golden and tastes like a quest. Because a bee makes a buzz, and that's a ringing in hir head sie can explain.

#

Yes. Jazz reminds you of a bee. Because a bee stings, and a sting is true evidence that you feel. How do you apologise to a biorobot you have created? In the world of research and engineering, apology is a hypocrite or a shadow or a make-shift desk with no authority. Apology is no answer for that which wants to come in and close the door behind it, leaving you trapped. Apology has no neat machine language, just a lisp. It might inhabit a name but casts adrift as a rowboat you swim and swim towards but can never reach it in your dream. Apology is a face in a hurricane, and it looks like your mother, drowning you. You look wrong and ridiculous questioning it, even drunk or alien, across a world of stories there and then, here and now.

You can't apologise, same way you can't tell your mae the truth. You live in two worlds, and you feel a deep and terrible sadness about that. When you leave each world, you carry boxes cramped with deception, trickery and guile encamped with sprites who make hostages from what matters. You're a god or a goddess who sows souls from shore to shore, fiddling away from chaos and grief. Swooping music vibrates in circles, rips and ripples, as the rest plod with sprites and souls, and the fiddle pecks, prods and cripples.

On a scale of 1–10, it feels like 0.

Before Jordan, you secured the walls of your heart so nothing new blew in, nothing old blew out. All that was left was reclaimed baggage occupying objects of memory never in use, simply recycled along undesignated revelations. What you needed was a blanket: washable, breathable, lightweight in summer, plush in winter. That blanket was Jordan. He saw through the flicker of light on the hourglass of your armour that suggested the straps were not made of steel but rather fairy floss. You were fragile, sickly sweet and poor for your health. You had only to let in Jordan, and everything changed.

You wonder why you didn't tell Jordan about the other dream. The one where your goddess walked with a gap across a city choked in smoke, and theories flew about the cavernous hole in her torso. Tar-shined ravens and death-watch beetles also soared through it. No one offered a mist blanket so she could fold her wings at midnight. She looked at herself and muttered a prayer or a dream. She gave anyone who looked an opus of her hollow.

#

Sie wears an infinite new coat over hir old coat. It's unrecorded, no assumptions. When summer. . . if summer. . . long days, dropping nights. When spring. . . if spring. . . Hir heart is sealed in envelopes to a city of new suns.

#

There's a deadness about the night, yet you pick at it. You feel a dirge inside, yet you're not good at chanting. You distract yourself with motion imagery from

Krema, Cyclone, Bash and Jazz in their routines around their meteorological stations. Krema—unmindful of pink flamingos, black jackals and fur seals only miles north in Walvis Bay—mono-focused on iron-coloured sand dunes in Namibia. Cyclone—neutral to calcareous caves and rocky waterfalls, ferns, even orchids and aroids of the sacred forest in nature's museum—collecting water and measuring rain in East India. Bash—impartial to salt flats, sand dunes, canyons, lakes and craters—simply charting dryness and windspeed in California.

I milked goats, says your mae in your head. *Took the produce, together with mangoes and tomatoes, to the stall in the market for your schooling.*

And I thank you, Mae.

Krema, Cyclone and Bash go about unquestioning of their lesser tasks, compliant that you will situate them to their higher purpose. But Jazz is different. As sie goes about hir climatological tasks in Antarctica, sometimes you notice a sadness in sie, and a happiness—the break of a smile, a spring in hir step—when sie integrates with nature. Sie sleeps under stars, swims in iced waters, gawks at penguins, feels snow on hir tongue.

You watch the screens. None of the biorobots can hear you and the hypersonic imprints of your invisible chant.

#

The place that reminds sie of home has deserts and seas. They scorch or hump in scars and pleas. Sie drags hir heart through heavens and earths in endless quests to find holy burghs. But what sie sees are memories and visas to the universe.

#

Jordan emails you a sample of his writing. "It's called 'Damned, More Than Thirty Percent'," he says. It reads:

Your body's flamboyant with tonight's headlines. An unruly bugaboo peers through the sight: X marks the spot.

You bob through the city, in, out of back streets, away on the freeway. But it's coming for you: the ghost of your harming. . . all glaring in half-light.

"It's called prose poetry," he says. "The rogue cousin of a poem and flash fiction. I wrote it for you—there's more in the head, Mazu. Think I'll make it big?"

"You'll be right."

"The text's spooky."

What spooks you more are your mae's words in your head: "Your children will do for you what you're failing me."

You fold away each memory of the old sun that's black frost, but can't escape it. Like the goddess in your dreams, you want new suns. You'd happily start again with no expectation of what's normal, each moment that happens.

CCTV, no popcorn. You look at the screen. This here is getting by. Is this how you want to live your life—getting by?

A bird on Jazz's screen catches your eye. It's running extremely fast on the ground, until it stops in front of Jazz. How the? In Antarctica? More so, you're fascinated by hir response to it. You watch with curiosity as sie reaches hir hand to the red-crested turaco.

#

It's green bodied, white-faced. It perches on hir shoulder. Sie hums. It screeches, jibbers, like a jungle monkey. They practice a shared language, something intuited from intrinsic selves. It's a wordless language cast from simple lives, complex to forget. But words never stay dormant long. They sear patterns in the snow, disrupt the icy water's rhythm. Jazz and the bird follow each other distances along the shore, hear voices in the wind, and they remember. It doesn't matter who speaks first. The turaco tells sie about luck and choice.

Sie hums.

#

It's grey and wet driving home. It feels like solstice, the longest and shortest day, all at once. The wipers go *lub dub lub dub* like a heartbeat. Or the sound of drowning.

What you get when you turn the handle and cross the threshold into your shared flat is a warm, sweet aroma of your mae's kitchen.

"I looked it up on the net. Got pumpkin leaves, cassava and curry from an African market in Clay. Drove miles to reach it. Sorry, no tilapia. I got a porcelain pot to bake it with chicken. Smells right, you think?"

"Always."

Jordan's smoky eyes put embers into your body, shimmers in all your senses. You hug him, notice base notes of wood, cypress and earth in his aftershave.

"How can you be taller than this morning when I left? What you been up to?"

He laughs. "You're not the only specialist around here. Writers do spells all the time. Know that?" His shoulders are broader, a few inches more. He carries them right, no big boy guns on his muscles—he goes easy in the gym. There's spunk in his boyish face, tenderness too when he looks at you, as he is now. "Think dinner can wait?"

Stroking fingers scorch away each longing for solitude and in its place blossom orchids into your heart. Luminescent stars, triple moons. You abandon independence and capitulate to the explosions of a galaxy inside your flesh.

Later, much later, you sit together on the high-rise balcony, smoking the city and its silver rain and blinking lights. Tonight, the metropolis has forgotten the taste of politicians and guile, traffic jams and disconnect. What it offers is the promise of morning dew. A new beginning.

You think about the biorobots. Already you know that Krema, Cyclone and Bash will graduate with soaring colours to the space research stations. Jazz—you don't know about sie. Jazz has excessive individual thought and, as a biorobotics engineer, you know there's one way to deal with that.

But sie's more than 1s and 0s. Sie's a spirit of age. Funny, it doesn't worry you now. It doesn't matter anymore about counterpoint, convolution or polyphony. So what? There's diversity in algorithms and intelligence, and what's wrong with difference? Would it be so foolish of you, perhaps, if you asked Jazz what sie wants to do with hir life? See what random sie comes up with.

#

Sie opens hir memories. Colour photographs tacked close to hir heart. Nothing in particular, just dirt roads to a day that's coming. It's full of songs and dragons. Sie's the one who sees ghosts, who walks on water in hir sleep. The child from a cerulean pearl yet smouldering with phoenix wings. Sie loves Daddy and his folding arms, the careful way his eyes chorus. Will the leaves bud, and the flowers open one by one? Sie walks in hir sleep, or is sie a ghost of hirself? There's no password to reset.

Thank you for sharing, jibbers the turaco. And never a ghost.

#

You miss the splendour of an African vista darker than tar. The starry nights and bush calls of the savanna. The moon's gaze on the regal height of baobab trees. You wonder how that would taste.

"Perhaps soon enough when you visit," says Jordan. You look at him, startled. "Speaking out loud, mate."

"Let's play *Imagine*," you say.

"You start."

"Imagine we're sitting in an air-loft garden atop a magellanic cloud orbiting the Milky Way," you say.

"Imagine the petal of a whirlpool flower wafting inward from an ultraviolet vista and reaching your soul," says Jordan.

"Imagine you're for life."

Jordan's smile is full of glitter. He feels like sunlight. You wonder if something this perfect could go wrong. He's the summer that gives you reason to wake each dawn. You tell him about Mae wanting you to marry, have children.

"I don't make much money," he says, dancing rays in his eyes. "I can't bear you any babies, but I can cook—that do?"

You join in his laughter, at first uneasy, then you settle into belly-deep mirth that pushes out tears in its high.

"Will you tell her?" Jordan asks, a glisten in his eyes too.

You look at him. "Righto. Tomorrow, I will." You clasp his hand.

"Ace."

"Would you—" you stammer at his raised brow, "like, maybe. . . I was thinking video call. . . like, um." The words rush out: "Shall we tell her together?"

"Sure thing. That's decent." He squeezes your hand.

"Serious?"

"I'm all in. A video is worth a thousand words, right?" The sun in his eyes.

"Dude, just don't kiss me."

Your laughter is together.

Now it's Jordan's turn to study you. "She'll pull through."

"You reckon? I've given so much. Surely, she can allow me this little happiness."

"Little?" He roughs you up, you roll on the floor giggling.

She'd be wounded, maybe mad. She might not speak to you for days, weeks, maybe months. But you'd send money, then you'd call. She'd tell you about how you were hard to come out, nearly killed her birthing you. How she didn't ask for the curse that closed her womb after one tiny child—look how you've grown. She'd get cunning, like a fox, go spiritual or ideological, tell you about so and so's daughter in the village. You'd distract her with the trickery of a hare, and gently remind her about Jordan.

The phone rings, and you let it. You stand at the balcony watching the road, as a silver sky in the vista reaches with its doubling rain. You hope that you'll dream many suns in all directions and a kaleidoscope panning out softly. That you'll sleep in late and wake in a tousle of toes and a smiling noon reeling towards Eden.

ABOUT THE AUTHOR

Eugen Bacon is a bi-demi African Australian author. She's a Solstice, British Fantasy, Locus and Foreword Indies Award winner, a twice World Fantasy and Shirley Jackson Award finalist, and a finalist in the Philip K. Dick and Ignyte Awards, and the Nommo Awards for speculative fiction by Africans.

Eugen is an Otherwise Fellow, and was also announced in the honor list for 'doing exciting work in gender and speculative fiction'. *Danged Black Thing* made the Otherwise Award Honor List as a 'sharp collection of Afro-Surrealist work'. She lives in the land of the Wurundjeri and Boon-Wurrung people of the Kulin Nation. Visit her at eugenbacon.com.

Integrated Learning

C.H. Pearce

"... group assignment..."

My head snaps up from the scratched desk I'm contemplating. My stomach drops like a stone. It's not like me to get distracted at the final hurdle. I tune into Teacher's drone.

Stonegate's classrooms are dark and damp. We have yellow, buzzing overhead lights, and beyond the windows, the tiertop of Level Two is lit with *more* overhead lights set to day-brightness to replicate the sun we don't get this far down the domed city. The classroom reeks of vinegar—evidence of a constant battle against mould. A small mushroom peeks out between the stone tiles by my black, buckled shoe. I resist the urge to prod it.

I despise group work. Everyone lets me down. The best I can hope for is a lazy parasite who will let me do all the work *right* and coast on my success. If they insist on interfering and dragging me down...

I need to ace this assignment. I'm on track to graduate with a perfect score and be initiated into the Select at the end of term. We're all the right age—eighteen—but of our class of twenty-eight, only Jas, Rena and I are still in the running.

No one will tell me exactly what happens when we graduate as Select, but the Select who come to speak at our school smile knowingly and tell me it is wonderful. Teacher isn't Select—god no, no Select ends up teaching squirts like us on the level they grew up on—but I see how he envies them. That's as compelling as imagining myself happy.

The Select go on to have exemplary careers on the upper levels—politicians, research scientists, medical specialists. Pull down the curtain, and

I'm convinced the Select are nothing but a cohort of nepotists, perpetrating an illusion of specialness. Who cares? It's a *meritocracy* of nepotists, and the criteria is academic perfection in school.

And little stick-up-the-arse, no-fun Gem from Level Two is going to be one of them. That'll show everyone.

". . . Gem, you'll be working with Max," says Teacher.

That's worse than group work.

I stand and stare at Max in horror at her desk across the room. She waves lazily and flashes me a snaggle-toothed grin. Max's eyes are heavy-lidded and she hasn't brushed her floaty blonde hair. It's matted at the back. Teacher says she'll be expelled if she doesn't clean up *by tomorrow*, but he's said that before, so I think they'll forcibly cut her hair like last time. She looks high. I wish she was, because she'd be more pliable. As it is, she's both stupid and stubborn, and thinks I should "chill out"—the worst combination in a partner imaginable.

"Sir." I raise my hand.

"Sit down, Gem. Working effectively with another personality without requiring intervention from a higher authority is part of the assessed component of the test. You *may* come to me with issues—but be aware this will lose you points. If you call on me, you will not get a perfect score."

I lower my hand. I sit.

I'm not a people person. That's part of the test. They saved the hardest until last.

I'm going to have to manage the assignment, and Max.

I take a deep breath. I can do this.

Teacher gives the others their topics. He comes up to Max and I last, and whispers our topic in our ears, separately.

#

"Integration of multiform hivemind organisms." I ambush Max at recess. "That's our assigned topic. I've heard about the Many."

Max sits on the low brick wall at the edge of the schoolyard, swinging her long legs. Black mould eats up one corner of the concrete.

There are new mushrooms sprouting in the cracks. It's only been a day since we carefully extracted the old crop, with our gloves and masks on, then burnt them.

Max takes a huge bite out of an apple. I watch her sharp right canine pierce the flesh. Juice dribbles down her chin.

She wipes her mouth with the back of her hand. "Want some?" she burbles with her mouth full, spraying me with flecks of apple.

I wrinkle my nose in disgust.

I *do* want a bite of her apple. And it might help to bond us if she feels she's done me a favour. I take it in my hand. The flesh gives unexpectedly under my fingers—it must be old, on the verge of rot. I still want some.

"Where did you get fresh fruit? No one sells it on Two." I take a bite.

It's meaty, oily. It's a Quickfat bar. The disconnect makes me gag.

"Your face!" Max giggles.

"Why imitation. . ?" I swallow, with difficulty. My eyes water.

"Makes me look posh." Max grins. She has gristle stuck between her teeth. "They're from the joke shop. Worth every penny. It's funny when people try to steal them. No one does it anymore."

I've bought Quickfat bars from town on our excursions with pocket money my parents sent me—and the slop we get from the cafeteria is the same mystery meat, fried or boiled to death. I just didn't expect it when I saw the apple. I don't like how Max throws me off balance. I twist my hands behind my back.

I clear my throat. "I want to talk to you about the group project. Leave the whole thing to me, and I'll let you take joint credit."

I put out my hand for a handshake.

Max licks oil off her fingers, one by one. I wait for her to take my hand, anticipating how disgustingly sticky it's going to be, but she doesn't. "Nah. I'm here to help. I'm no freeloader."

I frown. "Very well. Meet me at the library at lunch. I want a planning session. We'll see what materials the library has."

"*Relax*, Gemma." Max draws it out, and makes a popping sound with her lips at the end of my name.

"It's Gem."

#

I skip the cafeteria to head to the library at lunch. It's empty, except for the Librarian. I search the catalogue.

That's odd. I can't find any literature about multiform hivemind organisms I can access with my student ID.

I've never seen one of the Many. I hear they research them in the labs upstairs. The Select are probably publishing articles which haven't filtered down.

There is material listed in the catalogue—literature about the first appearance of the Many in the mid-21st century via a fungal organism in a fallen meteorite. The first human the Many absorbed. Anatomy, care and feeding, behaviour, reproduction, communication, and the Many's usefulness to humanity as a diplomatic partner and as a food crop grown and harvested on the upper levels. "The Many helped us thrive post-climate disaster in our sealed city. . ." reads one blurb. I wonder why we didn't study this in History.

There is one book in the Restricted section.

Max isn't here. It's been twenty minutes. She isn't coming—after insisting on helping!

I can't say I'm surprised.

I won't let it rattle me. Max and I are in the same dorm, and most of the same classes; she can't avoid me forever. My only task is to convince her to let me do all the work without interfering, then convincingly pretend we worked together. Everyone wins.

I ask the Librarian to see the book. She is sorting books by the front desk.

The Librarian frowns, with difficulty. Her face is inflamed, and one hand looks puffy under her shirtsleeve, because the state-sponsored cybernetic implants on her corneas and inset in her forearm keep getting infected. She only just got back from the last surgery. "Go to class. Don't speak of that book again."

I'm taken aback. Was I too abrupt? Should I have asked her how she was feeling, first? Or would that be too familiar?

"Are you feeling better, miss?" I try, wondering if I'm making it better or worse. I'm no good at this. I should have tried acting friendly *before* asking for the book. The Librarian and I see one another daily. I erred on the side of formality and never asked her name.

"I'm perfectly fine," says the Librarian, relenting. "The state pays to fix their own tech; the surgeries don't cost me anything but time and discomfort."

"Hopefully this time is the last," I say.

"I am assured—once again—that it will be. I meant what I said. My colleagues have been remiss in my absence—certain information isn't for young minds. You are not to speak of the matter again."

"Very well, miss," I reply reflexively.

If I want to read the book, I'll have to sneak in—tonight.

I've never broken Stonegate's rules before. I have a perfect record.

Would I break a rule to maintain that perfect record?

#

"Have you ever seen a Many?" Max whispers from the bunk above me in the dark. "Or is that *the* Many?"

"'One of the Many' is tidier." I blink at the slats above me. It's all shadows, save the light filtering through the gap under the door. I'm researching on the implanted tech discreetly set in my cornea and forearm, scrolling through academic journals, looking for articles on hive integration.

The electronic resources are behind a paywall, or blocked. There are social media posts, but they're no good to me. In any case, they are quickly redacted by the network's automatic censor.

My mind keeps circling back to the book in the Restricted section.

We're four to a room. Max usually sleeps in the top bunk opposite.

"Did you move bunks?" I frown. She's closer now.

"Chunyen graduated," Max says. "It was empty."

I liked it empty. I could think.

"So, have you ever. . ." Max presses.

"No, I have never seen one of the Many. No one here has. If everything goes right, and I'm accepted into the University and get a job as a researcher upstairs—*then* I will have the privilege of studying the Many."

"I've seen one," Max says.

I sit up in bed. I crane my neck to look up at her. "You haven't."

"Great big amorphous blob. Looked like grape flavoured jelly but fucken massive. With these fungal trails. . . like slime mould." Max wiggles her long arms wildly over the edge of the bed. "I saw it eat someone. Drew them in, like it wanted a hug, then *schloomp nom nom nom*. . ."

"You're lying." So why am I so interested?

Max sticks her head over the side of her bunk. Her long, frizzy hair trails down. "Got your attention though, didn't I?"

"If this was a physical book, I would throw it at you. Either leave it all to me, or listen to what I tell you. Show up when I ask. Then you'll have my attention."

"No, I won't. All you want is to be Select and buzz off upstairs and never see any of us again. You'll only tolerate me for as long as you need me." There's no malice in Max's words. Her long fingers with chewed-short fingernails drum the edge of her bunk.

"Don't *you*?" I counter. "Don't you want something more than this?"

I realise too late I've been insensitive.

Max purses her lips in a grim line. Max has already failed. Her scores are too low to claw her way back, even if she capped off her academic journey with a perfect score in our assignment. She's stuck on Level Two forever, at best. When we graduate from the institution she'll have to scrape by her own way.

"Let me brush your hair so you don't get expelled," I whisper, by way of apology.

"Pffbt. Teacher will chop it off like last time. Anyway, what difference would it make if I'm expelled?"

I would fail my last assignment.

My parents will be right to be disappointed in me. I'll never amount to anything.

Everything I've worked for—everything I've been publicly seen working for—will be for nothing. I'd thought I was being kind, but this isn't selfless. I need Max. "Come break into the Restricted section with me," I suggest.

It feels inevitable.

"Sweet." Max slides off the top bunk, and pads to the door—like she was waiting for my word.

We creep out without waking Rena.

#

The path to the Library is eerie at night. We use the soft blue light from our implanted tech to light our way—I'm worried the torchlight functionality would make us too conspicuous. The walk across the cold stones through the corridors, down the stairs, and through the courtyard seems to take twice as long as it does by day. Have I led us the wrong way?

The squat, stone block of the Library looms out of the darkness. It looks larger at night.

Will we set off alarms if I try the door?

"This was a bad idea," I whisper to Max.

I wish she'd give me a talking to. *You giving up on your dreams at the final hurdle is a bad idea, Gem,* and I'd reply: *You're right, Max, let's do this.*

Max shrugs. She scratches her stomach through her nightie and yawns. "Let's go back, then. Thanks for the night-time stroll."

"Follow me." I square my shoulders. I'm already standing ramrod straight.

I try the door. It's locked, but the alarm doesn't go off.

"Give me a boost, Max. I want to try the window."

Max helps me up. She's tall, and stronger than she looks, carrying me on her shoulders like a child, although she trembles with the effort of keeping steady.

I stretch up my hands. My fingers fumble on glass, feeling for the catch.

I push the window open. "Wait here." I haul myself up with difficulty.

I drop gingerly down onto the table on the other side. I make directly for the Restricted section. My heart is beating fast.

I pull the book from the shelf. I set it on the table and scan the pages on my eyeplant, flicking through quickly, trying to get all of it to pore over later. I don't want to take the book and get caught, and I don't want to linger here longer than we need to.

A photograph depicts a gelatinous, semi-opaque creature, about eight foot tall. The Many stands beside three smiling figures in white labcoats, two men and a woman, which help scale it. The Many towers behind them, tendril-like arms snaked around all three of them.

It's a workplace photograph. The caption reads *Michael the Many: A diplomatic milestone in human-offworld relations of 2205; the Facility for Extraterrestrial Studies is reimagined with its first former test subject on staff.*

The scientists' smiles are wide. Their faces have a wet, oily sheen. They look as happy as the Select who came to speak at our school.

I return the book to the shelf in the Restricted section and run back to the window to meet Max.

#

When we return to our dorm, Max creeps into my bunk beside me. "I want to see what's so great about this book," Max says.

I scroll through my scan, my forearm twisted to show Max my implanted tech. Max snuggles close and rests her head in the crook of my neck.

I find the workplace photograph. It will do Max good to see she was right about the rumour she repeated.

It's a black square.

Did I get the right page? It's the same caption. . .

Word after word is redacted before my eyes, a thick black strikethrough eating up the text.

I flick through more pages. Eighty percent of the text is struck through.

The network is automatically censoring the content, like with the social media posts.

"*No.*" I'm horrified.

"Get some sleep," suggests Max.

Max closes her eyes. She doesn't return to her bunk. By the time I prompt her, she's already snoring with her mouth open, drooling on my pillow.

#

In the morning, Max lets me brush her hair. It takes me half an hour to get all the tangles out with my fingers before I can begin to brush it.

"There you go." I admire my work, satisfied. I flatten her hair with my hands, because it almost immediately springs up again, and adjust her collar. My fingers graze her neck. I observe: "You have a freckle on the nape of your neck shaped like a heart."

"Want to kiss it?" asks Max.

"Um, not right now, thank you," I tell her politely—not knowing what I want, or what I should say. I think she's joking.

We have six days remaining.

By nightfall, I still haven't thought of anything better than *could I break in and see the book again?*

I suggest this to Max.

We sneak into the library in the night.

The book is missing.

I check the catalogue. The listing is gone, like the book never existed.

#

We have five days.

I've found no accessible literature in the library.

I've found no accessible literature material online.

I lie awake brainstorming furiously. I insisted Max return to the top bunk so I can think—or sleep.

The funny thing is that I must have gotten used to Max's company, because without her warm presence next to me, I can't settle. I keep scrolling.

I think about her lips and her chin, wet, after she ate the not-apple. The image is so vivid it almost frightens me. In my mind, Max's face is close—I can feel her warm breath.

I'm scrolling mindlessly, taking in no information. I feel prickly and overly warm. How much time have I wasted? Fifteen minutes? More?

"Can I get into bed with you?" Max whispers. "I had a bad dream."

I blush from head to toe. She can't *read my thoughts*. Thoughts don't mean anything at all—only action.

I clear my throat. I can't think of a compelling reason to say no. "Alright."

Max creeps under the covers next to me. I lie facing her.

Almost immediately, I relax. I think I could sleep.

"What was your nightmare about?" I whisper. I stroke her hair. It feels nice now I've brushed and untangled it, as delicate as dandelion fluff.

"A big fucken blob fucken eating everyone," whispers Max. She begins to giggle. "*Schhllooomp nom nom nom nom.*"

She kisses my cheek—I think—in an exaggerated way, wet and slobbering, pretending to eat my face, to an accompaniment of wet-sounding smacks and pops.

She climbs on top of me. She keeps her mouth on my cheek, so somehow I don't register until I'm half-winded under her weight.

I hate her for making it so easy I could open my mouth and kiss her, and afterwards pretend it was a game. I hate her for picking up on what I'd prefer to dismiss. I'm convinced she pities me. *Max* pities *me*! I'm the one who's going to get the hell out of Two, and give her and my parents a leg up after me. My face is burning. I feel weak.

"You lied," I snap. "You didn't have a bad dream at all. And you've never seen a hive. You're useless, and you want me and Jas and Rena to stay on Level Two with you and have equally shitty, pathetic lives so you're not alone. Well, I'm sorry for having ambitions."

Max goes dead quiet. She pauses with her tongue on my cheek.

Max rolls off me, then rolls over in bed, with her back to me. She takes the bedsheets with her.

"I'm sorry," I whisper. "I didn't mean it."

Max pretends to be asleep.

"I'm sorry, Max," I try again.

She's already snoring. Or—possibly faking a snore.

If I succeed, I could get Max out, too. Bring her upstairs with me. I could at least visit her. I wonder why that never happens. Maybe the Select think they're too good for their old friends once they're Selected. I wouldn't forget my friends on Two.

All the same, I can't bring myself to promise I'd always come back, in case I disappoint her.

#

I'm afraid I've ruined things with Max. I resent both of us for it. We have four days to do the assignment, so I need to patch things up today.

I want to explore the old science labs on the grounds. They might have salvageable textbooks, files, or information on old computers. The labs have been boarded up for years—since an incident the year I started at Stonegate, when twelve staff disappeared, which the remaining staff refuse to discuss—so any material will be woefully out of date. It's looking like my only shot.

I try to think of a way to make it up to Max, but by lunchtime in the cafeteria, I still can't think of anything.

I bring my tray and sit beside Max. I offer her a bite of my stale bread roll. There is a blossom of blue mould on the side of it. It's an empty gesture, because her meal is identical.

"Meet me behind the old labs in free period," I say. I hope desperately that she will say yes, despite our spat. I doubt the roll is a sufficient peace offering. "I'm sorry I was a personality bypass last night. Please say yes."

Max takes a bite of the roll, then stops. She chews thoughtfully. I wonder if it tastes mouldy.

Max grins hugely at me with her mouth full of pulpy bread. She nods.

#

I wait for Max behind the labs. They're corrugated iron demountables, blackened with mould, and ivied with creepers. The windows are boarded up. The front door is chained with a padlock.

The metal creaks, like it's shifting with a change in temperature. I hear scuttling from inside. I wonder how any animal got in.

Amongst the fat, white mushrooms at my feet, the ground is littered with cigarette butts.

This place isn't as abandoned as I thought.

Strong arms wrap around me from behind. They turn me to face them. I scream. Something warm and wet covers my mouth, muffling the sound.

It's Max, with her tongue down my throat, and both my hands in hers. She laces her fingers with mine, and presses right up against me with her lean, tall body. She laughs softly into my mouth. She backs me up against the hot, warped metal of the old demountable.

I'm letting her, why am I letting her? I'm surprised, I think. Her snaggletooth scrapes my tongue. I'm trembling. I open my mouth to hers and make a small, embarrassing sound. I'm trying to talk, but if she lets me, what would I say?

I want this, but not right now?

I like you, but I like my dreams more?

Look here, Max, this is how it's going to go—I become Selected, I keep it together, I bring others up after me. If I can't keep my head with you, what chance do I have with the Many—

Max pulls away. She rests one hand on the metal, leaning over me with a lopsided grin, until the metal gets too hot on her palm and she has to move her hand. Her other hand lingers on my hip.

I flush from the roots of my hair to my toes. I rake my hand through my hair. "I asked you here to help me with the project," I say.

Max crosses her arms. She looks like I've slapped her. "But this is where everyone comes to make out. And meet their boyfriends and shit."

"I didn't know that."

"Of course you didn't. I'm sorry, Gem. Do you still want to discuss the project?" she asks humbly, frowning at her shoes.

I open my mouth. No sound comes out.

The deadline is in four days. All I have from Max is her infuriating resistance towards leaving it all to me—I could do it alone, if she'd only support me and agree to pretend we're working together. Instead, she insists I accept her questionable "help" when she's going to make both of us fail.

I have her rattled enough to listen to my demands.

Every remaining minute is of the essence.

Why, then, do I stand there trembling, my lips parted, saying nothing?

"I want to break in and take a look around," I say eventually. "I brought bolt cutters and gloves."

Max nods. She wipes her mouth with the back of her hand. Two fingers linger on her lips. I try to put the feel of her lips on mine out of my mind. "Where did you get bolt cutters from?"

"The store room. Prefects have a key," I explain. "I'll return them straightaway when we're done."

I snip the lock. It takes more effort than I anticipated. Max sidles up behind me like she wants to help, then thinks better of it.

The chain falls away. I creak open the doors. They're rusted shut. I use my shoulder.

#

Inside, it's pitch dark, save the light filtering in from the open door.

We turn on the torchlight from our eyeplants.

It's a series of interconnected demountable buildings. There are long lab benches, littered with beakers and test tubes full of something rank—and papers.

Glass crunches under my shoes. The floor is thick with detritus.

The papers are less usable than I'd hoped. If they were books, they've been torn apart, mould-damaged, gnawed on, and at worst, composted. I pick out salvageable pages and pocket them, wondering how I'm going to cite them.

"Rats must have gotten in." I thumb a chewed page.

"Why are we whispering?"

"I don't know," I admit.

We creep forward. The back of the lab is dark beyond the reach of our torchlight.

In the back of the lab is a body. It's standing.

So why is my first thought that it is a body?

I grip the bolt cutters in my sweating hand. "Stand back."

I shine a light on the body.

It's a tangled mess of twelve bodies. The missing staff? They are decayed, almost skeletal. They are pinned to the wall, and to each other, by tendril-like fungal growth. The tendrils look dry and dead.

"Who did you hear the rumour from?" I whisper. "About the Many integrating people?"

"It was daft. Some old man in the joke shop. It was just a story," Max says.

I find her hand in the dark. I brush my finger against the back of her hand. She grips mine tight.

"This must have been the incident that caused the school to seal off the labs. I shouldn't have brought you here. I've exposed us to chemicals and god-knows-what." I'm seized with fear.

"I don't think so," says Max. She scratches her chin carefully with her elbow. "Looks like they died in the middle of an orgy. Not a bad way to go. That's what they wanted to cover up. Bunch of wrinkly old Teachers cooking up their own drugs and partying until it went wrong. Yuck."

"What makes you think that?"

"That one's on top of that one. Those ones are embracing." Max points. "Look at their faces."

I admit: "They look happy."

Their skeletal grins appear ecstatic—I could dismiss that. Their heads are thrown back. Their limbs are entwined.

I wouldn't end up like them. I'd use my advantages. I'd help Max. I'd know when to stop.

I lead Max out, with the few papers I can salvage. I shut the door and put the chain back on. Anyone who tries the door will see the padlock has been broken. I count on that happening after we've graduated.

#

Rena graduates.

Our class is whittled down to twelve.

It's only Max and I left in the dorm.

#

Over the next three days, I write the best paper I can with the evidence available to me. I cite each found fragment of scrap paper, the pages I recall from the book in the Restricted section, and quote the anecdote from the man in the joke shop. I don't directly reference the bodies, but I base my theory of integration into the Many on what we saw.

Max dutifully reads the paper.

Afterwards, she looks pale and shaky, like she's about to be sick.

"Put your electronic signature beside mine," I prompt. "We have a day to practice before we present it to Teacher."

Max swallows. "But you're not going to join the Select anymore. If you believe your own theory. You might be happy and successful, but increasingly, you wouldn't be you. Not that you couldn't be happy and successful here! You totally could. . ."

Max keeps babbling.

I take her hand and place it where I want it—on the tech inset in my forearm, over the blank space where her signature has to go.

"I know what I'm doing," I say, which is true.

"You have a plan. I knew you'd have a plan."

"I do have a plan."

Max nods. She signs. "Are you going to tell me what it is?"

"No."

She crawls into bed with me. She rests her head in the crook of my neck.

I tremble in her arms with the fear of working up to what I want to ask.

"Could you do your impression again?"

#

We present our paper in Teacher's office, with the door shut. The fireplace crackles.

Teacher smiles sadly, then burns it.

We get an A+.

"Are you sure you know what you're doing?" Max checks, on the other side of the door. She has that look again, pale and shaky, like she's going to be sick. "Not long till graduation."

"I know what I'm doing."

"Yeah, but—"

"What do you want to do in town?" We have an excursion pass. Our last.

#

We have hot chocolates together at a cafe in town. We act grown up. I feel happy and confident. At first it frightened me, being with Max, like I was losing myself—but I like it, and maybe I'm changing, but I don't lose myself, and I don't change my mind.

It's good practice. Integration is going to be just like being with Max. Every time I kiss her, or cuddle in bed, or argue, or get high, or watch her eat, or memorise her freckles, and find I don't fall apart at the seams, I'm reassured.

I won't lose myself. I won't lose sight of my goals. I'll manage it. I'll better myself and I'll bring her up after me, and then my parents, and they'll say all they believed in me all along even though none of them did.

#

I graduate as Select. Max claps and cheers with tears running down her cheeks.

#

We pack our suitcases.

INTEGRATED LEARNING

Children like Max don't technically graduate from Stonegate. They just melt away.

"Will you walk with me into town on your way to the station?" says Max flatly, like it's not a question. She holds a suitcase in each hand. One of them is mine. I can't help noticing that would make it difficult to part ways.

We're in plainclothes—our only sets. Max wears jeans and a t-shirt, and mine is a suit—hand-me-downs from our respective families.

I'm so pleased Max forgives me enough to talk to me. "Of course I'll walk you into town."

Max nods, without meeting my eyes. She walks ahead with the bags.

I ask: "What are you going to do?"

"Get a job in the joke shop," calls Max. "The owner's my dad's cousin."

"I'll come visit."

"No, you won't."

ABOUT THE AUTHOR

C.H. Pearce is an artist and an Aurealis and Brave New Weird Award-nominated and Ditmar Award-winning writer of horror-tinged speculative fiction. She's bi, quiet (but friendly, honest, say hi on social media), a fan artist, has a background in history and archives, and lives with her husband and two small children on Ngunnawal Country in Canberra, Australia.

Her short fiction has been published in *Body of Work* anthology, *Cosmic Horror Monthly*, *The Off-Season: An Anthology of Coastal New Weird*, and more. Find her work and links to social media on chpearce.net

Into Bitten Dreams

Matthew R. Davis

The two-seater leather couch against the window at the far end of the Redondo Room is empty when I clock on.

I start work at four thirty, a half-hour before the bar opens, and greet my co-workers. We quickly catch up as the four of us restock the fridges and snacks: Phuong's daughter has won another high school art prize, Hadrian has ended things with their latest squeeze and seems rather unruffled by it all, Carey is picking up some extra shifts at the infamous Crimson Candyland and insists it's just bar work. I have little progress to report and merely rehash some old news about job applications that are looking promising. This is no more true than it had been two months ago, but maybe repeating the lie often enough will twist fate's arm and manifest the truth.

An upmarket bar situated on the second floor of the Hadley Hotel, the Redondo Room is in fact perfectly square, an irony that only I seem to have noted during my months working here. The floors are polished wood, thousands of identical lengths laid in an intricate houndstooth pattern, but that's the only aspect that betrays any real thought or taste: the corners are manned by potted palms, the brutally functional tables alternate between higher types that require a stool and lower ones that tend the booths, and the DJ role is usurped by a randomised playlist of bland trip hop that switches to a medley of modern pop hits at eight o'clock sharp. The fixtures are clean and pristine, the craft beers on tap pricey and the wine list even more so—but overall, the place makes so little impression on me that I have my own name for it.

"Another night of awe and wonder at the Redundant Room," I murmur to Carey as she bends to the glass washer.

"Well, it's five o'clock somewhere," she says, unleashing a cloud of steam and revealing a batch of hot wet pint glasses. "Might as well be here."

I check my phone, swift and discreet—Hadrian can be a real bear about mobiles on shift. "Not just yet. But oh, look, they ignored the sign again."

Carey glances over her shoulder as she straightens with a tray of fresh glasses, her smirk hidden from the newcomers who have ignored the standing CLOSED sign as if it were a loitering beggar. "They're just keen to see you, Brae."

I flick her with a towel. "Reckon you're more their speed, you indie waif."

The first customers are a clutch of real estate agents from up the street, their blue sports coats immaculate and the creases in their fine trousers razor-sharp. They are followed by another group from the surveyor's office, all pencil skirts and heavy foundation with too much bronzer, and then all four of us are hard at work, opening wines and fetching glasses and pouring pints. The patrons are intent on their own conversations and pay little attention to the people serving them, which I hate but also prefer to their chummy sense of entitlement when they do attempt to engage the staff in conversation or, as often, complain about something.

I'm often amazed that I've found myself here, flying from customer to customer, handing over EFTPOS devices and taking them back tapped. My life has been hard-knock from the get-go, a daily gauntlet run I've survived by the skin of my teeth, and yet I've landed a plummy casual gig serving at one of the city's better hotels—but that, of course, just puts me at the beck and call of the casually affluent, people whose idea of a teenage crisis had been a matter of which future CEOs to suck up to rather than the question of whether belt or razor would be the less painful terminus. The people who frequent the Redondo Room work in industries that have made my own life harder—driving up property prices so that the notion of ever owning a home has become a distant pipe dream, for instance—and that makes me bristle with resentment beneath my carefully maintained customer service façade. Sometimes, the anger boiling behind that composure feels so potent that I'm surprised it doesn't sour the wine I'm serving to vinegar.

Ah, but you know, whatever. Life is a bitch, everyone knows that, and most of my friends are bitches, too. At least I have them to look forward to as my second hospitality shift of the day limps toward its inevitable end. The Redondo Room will close at ten tonight, sending its patrons downstairs to drink with the riff-raff and giving me fifteen minutes to clean up before clocking off—just short of the span that would allow me a break or extra pay for not taking one—and then I'll meet a group of outrageous fellow hospos at a little boho bar up the street for a post-work drink. That's dangerous, a temptation to spend too much of the money I haven't been paid yet, but I've always liked to skate close to the edge. I've fallen off it once, what hold can it have over me now?

I brush aside a temptation to touch the old wound and pour another drink, store another receipt. Not here, if I can help it—but what *doesn't* help is the word tattooed on my left hand, running up to meet my index knuckle. *Nicolette*, a name with a decade and a half attached to it, all hanging off the hook of one terrible week. I'd put it there to remind myself of the best of her, but it's one end of a short fuse... and every time my eyes fix on those nine letters, I have to stamp out a sudden spark before it races through to the ugly explosion at the other. Of all my tattoos, that's the one I'd get covered up if I could afford it. At least it's on my left hand, so I don't have to see my mother's name every time I jack off.

The couch across the room from me is still empty when the post-work rush dies down and I take a quick toilet break. There have been nights where I'd have a discreet little snort or taste to get me through the unending series of punishing shifts at multiple venues, but I've been a good boy lately and do nothing worse than fail to pick up a balled paper towel when my indifferent toss misses the bin. I check my hospo WhatsApp group for messages—Jake is trying to convince everyone we should go see The Oopizootics tonight and Ollie is firing off hilarious invective about the customers at his bar every fifteen minutes. As I pocket my phone, my eyes drop to the paper towel on the floor, crushed into a defensive curl like an abused child, and the longer I look at it, the more it seems to take on the weight of my wounds. Away from the world's prying eyes, I find myself unable to resist stroking old scars.

Nicolette raised me alone, and whilst I resent the dumb name she lumbered me with, I've always appreciated the considerable efforts and stresses she took aboard on my behalf. We were close enough that I'd almost come out to her at fifteen—assuming her motherly instincts hadn't been picking up the signals for years—but then, as I'd wrestled with my identity and what it meant for my future, she'd fallen deathly ill. Her hospital room didn't feel an appropriate time or place to talk about myself, so I just held her hand and wished for the impossible. My needs and truths could wait, and if Nicolette never knew, well, that meant there was no chance she could re-evaluate her son and see less than she had before. She waxed liberal and wore rainbows, but certain things had a funny way of becoming undesirable when they got right up close to you. I said nothing.

Words, or their lack, didn't matter in the end. My mother may or may not have recognised me for what I was, but at least one person did.

Damien.

Stung, I push myself away from the sink, check myself in the mirror, and slide my work face back on. I do my good deed for the day by popping the discarded paper towel in the waste bin as I leave the bathroom to resume my place behind the bar, and that's when I notice that the two-seater leather couch against the window on the far side of the room is now occupied.

A pair of women sit there, bare legs crossed, their faces hidden in shadow as the last blood of sunset drains away in the window behind them. Model-tall and clad in sleek black satin cocktail dresses, their long fingers cup wineglasses half-filled with a sanguine red. My interest in women is aesthetic at best, so I dismiss them from my mind as I turn back to serving ruddy real estate agents with more teeth than charm.

"Tin and jonic, thanks," quips one, following up with a fake laugh so well-rehearsed it has become instinctive. "Don't worry, I'm not drunk. Yet."

When I started here, my friends joked that I'd be well-placed to pull some moneyed men, and I'd thought so, too. I was flirted with a couple of times, and that was welcome, but the appeal quickly palled. I don't fancy being someone's bit of working-class totty, feel insulted at the thought that some of these men would consider any affections bestowed to be a privilege—one they extend with the easy hand of someone who understands little of true value. Yeah, it would just be a quick shag or a brief fling, but the imbalance in such a relationship unnerves me. And that response is warranted when you consider the object lesson I learned in high school.

Damien had been a couple of years older, out and proud and handsome as any football star and/or future real estate agent, butch enough to be accepted by his straight male peers and bitch enough to be admired by his female ones. Damien saw right through my thin skin to the secret unfurling beneath, and one of my darkest days was brightened when he extended an invitation to sit with him at lunch. Lonelier than I'd ever been as my hospitalised mother slipped further away each day, I was thrilled to gain the attention of such a strapping young god. We talked all through the break period, and then Damien set my heart galloping with the suggestion that we meet after school. That last class was an eternity of agony that I passed by thinking impossible things until it was over. We met in a nearby park, furtive as spies about to exchange explosive intel, and then we walked back to his house—

"Brae?" Hadrian. "Pass us another till roll, mate."

The demands of a busy job are a godsend sometimes, leaving me little time to think. I concentrate on serving until the bar falls quiet and Hadrian asks me to do a quick glass collection. A standing table in the middle of the room has been abandoned, left littered with ice-clumped empties and dreg-heavy bottles, so I head to it and start to pile up the remains.

I'm halfway to the other side of the bar now, almost dead centre, and that gives me a clear view of the couch against the window. Those two women are still holding court there, and though I've seen no-one approach to petition them, the way they sit almost seems to invite it. No, more than petition. . . supplication, perhaps. They're identical for all intents and purposes, their long legs crossed in opposite directions like a mirrored image, both wearing jaw-length hair that might have glowed blonde if the room were less dim. And that's the thing that brings me up short for a moment, because whilst the lighting in the Redondo Room is lowered for atmosphere, I can't see the women's faces at all. Maybe it's because they're backlit by the heliotrope sky and heavy shadows of a dying sunset pressed against the window like a grimly psychedelic oil show, but all I can discern is their pendulum-blade smiles. They bare strong white teeth like a warning to the world.

I blink myself back into service and carry away a leaning tower of glassware. They're just *people*, and by their presence and carriage, well-off ones—my least favourite breed. All that should disturb me is the fineness of their bedsheet thread count compared to mine, the undoubted ease of their daily existence.

They probably slide through life like it's been oiled and perfumed for them, slick as eels. Oh, I know women have their own set of troubles to navigate through life, but *these*. . . these two radiate the impression that nothing so frail as a glass ceiling could contain them, that they stalk giant-high through the city's neon nights like *kaiju* in cocktail dresses, crushing all opposition under designer heels. If they uncrossed their legs, perhaps I'd see sets of strong square teeth grinning in there too. All the better to eat you with, my dear.

Ah, but I'm getting fanciful again, I tell myself as I deliver the glasses to the sink where Phuong is slicing lemons and limes with her usual brisk efficiency. Vagina dentata, really? I thought maneater clichés went out with #MeToo, when we all became a little more aware of the world's dietary balance. True, I often indulge in cynical and exaggerated fantasies about other people—but then, I've spent most of my life trying to escape one thing or another, so hopping into someone else's head makes for a useful distraction. Especially when bad memories keep popping through the soft skin of my awareness like broken bones.

Or hard white teeth.

The bar is still in a quiet patch, Carey serving as the others clean up, so I grab a cloth and wipe down my end of the counter. My eyes land on my hand, *Nicolette*, and skip away—but too late. The fuse is lit, and tonight I feel unusually vulnerable to the past, unable to stop that flame from racing to its conclusion.

Damien's house, that monumental night. Welcomed into the warm den of his room, accepted and safe, I had been unable to keep from revealing the truth of my sorry situation. . . and Damien, he *understood*. Oh, he'd never lost a parent—his were on their biannual month-long holiday, this time in the

Seychelles—but he knew how a confused young man could feel so alone. He knew the value of affirming company. Strong shoulders. Warm arms.

I lost my virginity on Damien's bed that night. Everything I'd thought of whilst frantically flogging away under the covers as Nicolette slept, everything I'd read about or heard tales of or seen in porn, was made stunning reality by my new friend. The world opened up, and there was a light inside, and that light was soft and gentle and hard and tearing but it accepted, and it embraced, and it loved. I felt like I had discovered God.

And then I snuck home early the next morning to find Uncle Ernie and his partner Ksenia waiting on my doorstep.

A raucous laugh brings me out of my reverie, and I snap a glance toward its source, suspicious as always that I am somehow the cause of amusement. A boozy boomer in a loosened tie is slapping the shoulder of his compadre, as unaware of my existence as could be. Behind him, one of the younger estate agents is ambling toward the couch against the window, bearing a beer for luck. Finally, one of these strutting roosters has summoned the audacity to approach the tenebrous twins.

The man is wearing a taupe sportscoat and tight fawn slacks, wingtip brogues balancing the jut of his expensive haircut. He's perhaps thirty, handsome in a promising-young-footballer-now-slowly-going-to-seed kind of way, the kind of guy who might seek to impress you with the fidelity of his home stereo by spinning a classic Beastie Boys repress still fresh from its wrapping. In my experience, these dudes are invariably straight and inordinately successful with the women swimming their end of the pool, and this one maybe figures he's found some lucky new beneficiaries of his worldly knowledge. I hope those faceless women wield their knowing grins to put the guy right back in his place.

I have the strangest feeling they will, and maybe it's just a little schadenfreude to ease the constant ache of my own life, but I want to see it happen.

This privileged paramour comes to a halt before the couch, blocking the women from my view. I see his free hand articulating a confident opening line, and then a middle-aged office manager in chunky wooden jewellery totters my way with her glass held out like a votive offering. I swallow a sigh of frustration and refill her with red.

"Ah, you're a lifesaver," she sighs, and I smile my professional smile, holding the EFTPOS pad out to her. I take a moment to enjoy tearing off the transaction receipt and impaling it on a short spike, and then the tell-tale crash of smashing glass brings my head snapping up.

The taupe peacock is now facing toward the bar, frowning quizzically at the spray of jagged shards fanning out from between his brogues. I wonder if he was shut down hard by his intended targets and spun around to leave in a petulant tizzy, dropping his beer as he did so—the women certainly seem amused by his mishap, their smiles undimmed. But if that's the case, the man's slighted pridefulness has disappeared with the shattering of his glass, leaving him with a look of befuddlement as though he's snapped into sudden sobriety after hours of senseless inebriation. He glances blankly at us behind the bar, shrugs off any responsibility, and wanders away toward the exit without a single glance back at the couch and its inscrutable occupants.

Hadrian sighs. "Brae, would you do the honours?"

"On it, boss." I fetch a cloth and dustpan, abandon the safety of the bar. The other patrons offer their fellow little more than an amused glance and a few inevitable cries of "Taxi!", already forgetting the incident. The centre of the room is clear, and I make quick work of the breakage. I sweep the jagged fangs of glass into the pan's waiting mouth, wondering how difficult it would be to glue them all back together and make the vessel whole again. Almost impossible, surely, and even then, the result would be unfit for any practical purpose. . . and if a simple glass is doomed by damage, what hope can broken people have?

My mind shoots off its tether as I wipe the floor dry. *Nicolette.* Damien. And everything that comes along after them.

Uncle Ernie and Ksenia waiting on my doorstep.

They'd been trying to call me, but I'd been distracted by last night's raunchy revelations and my phone had gone flat. I didn't need them to say anything—the looks on their faces, the raw red of their eyes, told me all. Something inside me ruptured and my body was filled with a strange, anarchic energy I'd never known before, an electricity that could have propelled me over rooftops if only it hadn't turned inward to paralyse my trembling frame. The world somehow kept spinning, sublimely unaware of its latest loss, and I began to understand the true meaninglessness of life.

Officially orphaned, I skipped school and went home with Ernie and Ksenia. I brought my needful things with me, because they didn't want me left alone in the flat at such a time. They didn't ask where I'd been all night, for which I was grateful in the extreme. How could I possibly have told them that I'd been sucking my first cock as my mother died alone and unwitnessed?

Though I'd had time to brace for it, the absence of Nicolette was chilling, absolute. I'd never spent much time with her quiet labourer brother Ernie and his Russian beautician lady, had never bonded with them, and that meant I could barely talk to them about all the ways I hurt. And so they were there with me, but I was alone. I had no-one.

Except Damien.

After an endless night of sorrow and guilt, I *needed* to see him with an urgency I'd never known before. Wondrous memories of our explorations together had been all that kept me from buckling under the strain of loss; even though I felt I'd betrayed Nicolette by abandoning my vigil—like she wouldn't have died had I been there holding her hand—I couldn't bring myself to wish I'd passed up that blissful time with Damien to be with her instead, which only made me feel worse. I went back to school aching with a desperate desire to grasp what I had been offered and use it to claw my way out of the mire.

And Damien brushed me off like shit on his shoe.

I learned another lesson about pain that day, an invisible blade pushing somehow deeper into my heart as Damien joked with his *real* friends about how he'd picked up another lovesick puppy. The torrent of words I'd planned to unleash dammed up my throat, so I just stood there and trembled as Damien revealed the truth of himself. I saw my sorrow and my soul had meant little to my seducer; it pleased him to worm his way into uncertain confidences and virgin bodies, finding sport in those who would admit him with all the gravity of first love and offer up cherished prizes he saw as no more than trinkets. Damien was a shallow, manipulative narcissist who skated by on good looks and cruel, fickle charm, and to him, little Brayden Haney was nothing more than the latest salacious escapade in his endless war against boredom.

Another lesson learned, then: I had assumed I was safe amongst my own kind, only to find that queerness was no guarantee of personal integrity. As Ollie liked to put it: *arseholes transcend all borders.* These days, I can admit that some of the worst people I've ever met are gay . . . but at the time, this understanding came as one crippling blow too many. My mother's death had been a mortal wound; Damien's betrayal was the *coup de grâce*. The pain blotted out everything else.

That evening, I walked back to the park where I'd met Damien, two days older and two tragedies wiser. I went there alone, and I did not intend to return.

Later, I would learn that my own dark sense of humour had given me away: I'd left the house with a simple but loaded "I'm just gonna go hang", a line whose delivery bothered Ksenia so much that she convinced Ernie they should follow me. Thanks to her intuition, they were in time to save me from my own designs, for my uncle—still in his dirty labourer's cargo pants, a workplace blade in his pocket—to cut me free of my makeshift extension-cord noose before my premature departure became permanent.

The resulting shame had been every bit as excoriating as the pain. Not only had I failed to kill myself, I'd put Ernie and Ksenia through a terrible ordeal right on the heels of a devastating loss. But though I expected them to berate me for my selfish choices, they actually said very little. They let *me* talk. And they gave me space to heal, a place in their home to call my own, without ever expecting me to be anything other than myself. I was stunned and humbled to realise that Uncle Ernie, whom I'd assumed to be boring, none too bright, and probably homophobic, was in fact patient and thoughtful and *kind*. And sweet, funny Ksenia—whom I'd made the butt of mail-order bride jokes to my classmates—was his harmonious match in every way. The pair of them never judged me unfairly, never made me feel othered. They called me out on my behaviour when I deserved it, but they treated me less like the child they'd chosen not to have and more like an equal who just needed a little room to move and guidance to grow. Ernie and Ksenia saved my life—not just that night in the park when the shadows had run deep as oblivion, but slowly, consistently, over and over again.

Unbelievable, perhaps, but something *good* followed Nicolette's death: I came to know my remaining family and found love where I had expected casual affection at most. My heart is a hard nut to crack, but their unconditional kindness has earned my eternal loyalty a dozen times over. In the bad times, thinking of Ernie and Ksenia is like watching the fuse burn in reverse, the exploded pieces of my past drawing back together and fitting into place. The whole is not perfect, and some bits will always be jagged or missing, but I've learned better lessons from the healing than I did from the wounding, and I know that a broken glass well-mended is worth the keeping.

I stand, sighing at these unbidden memories as I tilt the dustpan to keep the splinters of glass from falling back on the floor, and movement catches my eye.

The women on the couch are beckoning to me.

Their free hands wave me over in unison, a motion perfected through repetition, and I prepare my usual line: *sorry, you'll need to come to the bar for service.* But as I cross the houndstooth floor to stand before them, assuming the place of the estate agent whose mess I've just cleaned up, I find the professional admonition dying in my throat.

I still can't see their faces. How is that possible? The discreet downlighting of the Redondo Room should cast no pall over them, yet their features are obscured by shadow. Only their smiles cut through, the gleam of their teeth. Their bodies are distinctly visible, from the fashionable talons that hold their wineglasses with mannequin-perfect poise to the shaven sheen of their long, crossed legs, but they are ultimately anonymous. Uncanny, even, like a picture that looks a little too good not to be an AI fake.

Unreal. That's the word that springs to mind, but in a matter of seconds I come to understand this is not the case at all. They are something I've always *assumed* to be so, and the longer I stare at them, the more I wish there were anything artificial about this intelligence. Any lie, any blissful ignorance would be preferable to the immutable *fact* of their baleful presence. But obliviousness is no longer an option now that they have shown themselves to me, now that they allow me to understand the merest hint of a reality far beyond reason.

Staring into their hypnotic grins, I realise why my worst memories have been brought to the surface time and again tonight. I understand what dire magnetic force has pulled them free.

And I know *why*.

I hadn't been far wrong before, when I imagined these two stomping through the city like titans. They wander where they will and they take what they choose. The world is their veldt, but they are hunters of more discreet meats than most predators; they don't collect skulls as trophies, but rather what lurks within them. Delicious deviances. Toothsome trauma. The bloody gobbets of emotional evisceration. Pain brings them like chum shovelled into water, and I am a walking bucket of berley.

Here, then, are the sharks.

The din of the Redondo Room fades to a dull throb, redundant indeed, and my peripheral vision bleeds away. I'm barely aware of holding something but have already forgotten what that is. I see only what is before me, nightmares masquerading as women, and of them, all else pales or palls beside their smiles. Those *teeth*! How had I ever thought these two to be just another pair of punters? Their grins are as far from kind as it is possible to be. They are cruelty incarnate. They are hunger writ immense. And they will not, *cannot* be denied.

I watch, paralysed, as hell uncrosses its legs and rises from the couch in perfect symmetry. I'd laugh if I could at my earlier fantasy of vagina dentata, knowing now that these things are teeth all the way through, but I'm too stunned to speak and they *keep* rising. I'd thought them statuesque before, but now they loom over me as though I'm an infant, their blonde heads brushing the high ceiling of the bar, and yet their hungry smiles leer closer as if independent of those cyclopean bodies. The teeth don't part until they are all I can see, and even then I catch only the briefest glimpse of what lies behind them, but that is torn from me by the dizzying agony of violent disassociation as they bite into my mind.

It feels like, sounds like, breaking glass.

"Brae!"

I come back to myself slowly, a strange return of awareness that I equate with recovering from oxygen deprivation—I can almost feel the extension cord around my neck. Someone is laughing, someone is crooning a pitch-corrected psalm of love, someone is saying my name. Phuong grasps my elbow, frowning up at me with concern. Why? I look down and see a dustpan on the floor, a spritz of shining shards scattered around it.

"Are you all right?"

"I. . . I think so? What happened?"

"I don't know! I heard the glass breaking and saw you looking like you were about to faint." Phuong glances over at the bar, where our colleagues are no doubt watching with curious concern. "You okay? You been sleeping?"

"Not on the job," I tell her, rubbing at a tender spot on my head. No, *inside* my head, beyond the reach of my probing fingers.

"Ha ha. You work hard and play hard, but you need to *rest* hard, too. Young people! Always think you're invincible. Come sit down for a minute."

Phuong leads me behind the bar, where Hadrian has prepared a milk crate for me to sit on and a set of OH&S questions for me to answer. Carey brings me water, then seems to realise I can't be trusted with glass and holds onto it, hovering in concern. Something about the way her teeth nip at her lips makes me avoid looking at her.

"I'm fine, I just. . . I don't know, I don't feel well. Don't worry about me. You need to water the horses."

This phrasing brings out a rash of frowns on my workmates, but they take the point and return to serving. I can feel patrons eyeing me and try to ignore the grubby prodding of their gazes. I have to buck up, get through the shift—as a casual employee, I'm not entitled to sick leave and won't get paid for any hours I miss. How much longer until I can crawl away and die?

I slip out my phone. Just past nine, an hour left on the clock—I can manage that. Jake has posted another message in our Whatsapp thread; I open it, see it's directed at me. *WHAT UP SLUT! U WORKING WE DRINKING! FYL.* Jake has attached a photo of he, Ollie, and Desmond at our favourite booth, a rushed selfie that severs their heads halfway up. All I can see below the top edge of the picture are three toothy grins.

I gasp and spasm, dropping the phone on the floor before it can swallow me. My heart races as I trace my evening back a few minutes and remember what brought on my dissociative episode. I flinch again as those smiles bite deep into my being, just as I had when I'd looked at the group photo, my mind flashing white with the gleam of exposed teeth.

Despite my intention to soldier on, I'm quick to agree when Hadrian suggests I head home and get some rest. I pick up my phone, rise gingerly to my feet, and say my goodbyes.

The two-seater leather couch against the window at the far end of the Redondo Room is empty when I clock off.

#

It seems that life's lessons will never cease, for I learn several new ones over the following weeks.

An example: wearing a band-aid on my finger is a wise course of action, at least until I can get into a tattooist's to have a cover-up done. For something has changed within me; a sequence has been rewritten. Whenever I glance at my naked finger now and see my mother's name, the fuse burns faster than ever: *Nicolette*, Damien, the park—*teeth*.

Always they wait for me at the end of that train of thought, a gaping gullet at the end of the funhouse tracks, a flash of pale terror tearing through the wet web of my mind. I can no longer think of my mother, or my first lover and betrayer, without seeing the teeth. They bite me inside as I remember those women-who-weren't, the truth they showed me, and understand what they have taken from me in return—all in a flash, the same time it takes me to spasm as if shocked. That chain of memories has become a livewire that I dare not touch and yet cannot avoid.

I do what I can to minimise this trigger. I quit my job at the Redondo Room in case those fiends returned there, but also because seeing that couch would set me off every time my eyes fell on it. I fight for more shifts at my other casual hospitality jobs, coping with the intense schedule by leaning on narcotic crutches I'd been so diligently avoiding. My mind is a blank slate, my body a machine going through well-rehearsed motions, but that is just what I want. I need to not *think*. I cannot let myself remember the truth of the wider, weirder world.

Implacable, however, it seeps into my hours of rest and infects my dreams. Every night, no matter how medicated, I find myself caught in the melting tar of my thoughts, assailed and devoured by horrors. . . and though I can never quite remember them, a hint is always waiting. I explode awake and every time, the moonlight catches and shines upon something—the water glass on my bedside table, the screen of my phone, a patch of clear white wall—and I think it's the *teeth*, back to bite me so deep and grievous, and I spasm in fright. Just for a second, and then gone—but always with me, always.

It never is the teeth when I wake in the dark of my room, sweating and sobbing over dreams I can't recall and memories forever tainted with the shining spit of something inconceivable—not yet. But I know, as certainly as if I'd been told, that one of these nights when I burst out of sleep's poisoned embrace, *they* will be waiting. My blood is in the water now, running from countless toothsome wounds, and their bite is worst of all, too deep to ever heal. Soon, there will be no glass, no screen, no wall—only the awful inevitability of game run to ground. Forms faceless as shadows come to batten on my past, and teeth as bright and terrible as truth.

ABOUT THE AUTHOR

Matthew R. Davis (he/him, cishet ally) is a Shirley Jackson Award-nominated author and musician living in Adelaide on Kaurna land, with over one hundred short stories and six books published to date. His latest is *The Cure On Track: Every Album, Every Song*, with his next horror collection *Songs of Shadow, Words of Woe* and his novelisation of the Australian indie film *Ribspreader* coming later in 2025. He shares his life with the award-winning artist Meg Wright, aka Red Wallflower, and her cats Juniper and Lexi. Find out more at matthewrdavisfiction.wordpress.com.

Tattermog

Louise Pieper

I took from my childhood a wooden spoon, a goat, and a long, long list of flaws. Someone was always willing to say what was wrong with me. Not my mother, who disappeared when I was six. Not Magi, my twin sister, who loved me as I was. And not often my father, who kept to his tower doing whatever it is that wizards do.

Mostly, it was the village women who came and went like bustling hens. They'd climb the sixty-seven steps to our mountaintop home and cluck and clean and cook and twitch their fingers in ward signs when the shadow of Father's tower touched them. They praised Magi with a catalogue of virtues— she was good and kind and beautiful, and I was. . . not. They said that, when we were born, I had come bawling and brawling into the world, red-faced with rage, and announced to my horrified mother that the next twin would be more to her liking.

Poxwhallop! I was a precocious child, but not that bad.

It was true that Father preferred Magi. He gave her the clumping name of Magimerismara, like pinning a banner to her dress that said she was a wizard's daughter and not to be trifled with. He gave her a ring of jade and a caged bird to amuse her. He called me Tattermog and shoved a wooden spoon in my mouth when I wailed too loudly while cutting a tooth. Still, I had the best of it. The jade ring shattered and kind-hearted Magi freed the little bird. I kept the spoon, to pin up my hair, and no-one cared if a girl called Tattermog was wild and reckless and made friends with the mountain goats.

TATTERMOG

When the village women weren't listing my flaws, they would tell us tales of our father's wizardly might. He'd commanded giants to build his castle high in the Tangjat Mountains and smashed the king's army with storms and stones, when they'd ridden to see who dared claim the peaks. The king of Alatay had raged and Father had laughed. Long before, he'd found a way to imprison his death, and since it couldn't find him, he couldn't die. The women said he was the greatest wizard who'd ever lived and that he'd live forever.

He was not so great that he thought to make a place where two little girls might feel at home. The only part of the castle not as grey and bleak as Father's gaze was a walled garden with a spring-fed pool that was the source of the Otysh River. Beside it, three trees hung over a grassy bank. From the pool, a rill ran to the garden wall where a missing stone let the water leap free. It skipped and chuckled down the mountain, merry as a sprite child, joining hands with other streams to flow on to the sea. Tucked in against the rocks and behind the trees, a withy gate opened onto the castle's stone steps.

The village women slipped in through that gate rather than climb another dozen steps and face the dire portal of the wizard's iron-bound castle door. I slipped out through the gate to ride Barleycorn, my favourite goat, over the crags. Magi would sit by the pool, tickling the fish or reading tales. None of us liked that the shadow of Father's tower would sweep across the garden like a bird of prey, spying on us all.

One day in our twelfth summer, when I lay on the grass, exhausted from riding and romping, I said, "Magi, I've been thinking—"

"Oh, we're in trouble." She laughed and plucked a thistle from my tangled hair.

"Remember the songs our mother sang?" I asked.

"Not really." Magi drifted her hand into the water and giggled as a silvery fish rose to nibble her fingertips. "It's been six years. Do you think she'll ever come back?"

"Harkslops! You don't believe that old tale?"

"I don't believe she died of a fever." A frown rippled across my sister's face. "We'd remember that, surely. Maybe a minstrel did come to the village and sing with a voice so lovely he lured her away. Maybe—"

The shadow of the tower covered us and Magi clenched her hand. The fish darted away. Father did not like us to speak of our mother but when we were alone, I kept talking.

"Maybe she wanted to leave this place." I dragged my spoon from my hair and shook it at the tower. "But I don't think she did."

Magi shivered and wrapped her arms around herself. "Hush, Mog," she cautioned.

"She used to sing about this garden."

"La, la, la, my little. . ." Magi trailed off, glancing around for any sign of the shadow. "No, I don't remember it."

"Bothersox, you don't! She likened you to this pretty, golden pear and me to this tough old fig, dark and ugly—" I went on over her protest, "—but sweet enough on the inside."

Above us, the branches of the nut tree rustled although the rest of the garden was still.

"She never mentioned a nut tree," I said. We both looked up at the murmuring branches and then down at the tree's dark roots. "I don't think it was here. And in all the years we've played beneath it, has it ever borne a nut?"

"Mog," my sister whispered, "Father says not to trifle with wizards."

"Solspiddle!" I snapped my fingers to show how much I cared for what Father said and sang softly, "Sleep my pretty little fruits: my baby fig, my golden pear. Bless your leaves, your trunks, your roots. Far sweeter crop than trees can bear."

The nut tree shivered and then we froze, Magi and me and the tree, as the light dimmed in the garden again. I gasped a breath of air, cold as spite, and forced out words I knew would scare off our watcher.

"Barleycorn is fighting over the nanny goats on the mountain again, but he's twice as strong as the other billies, and his horns—"

The shadow shuddered and moved on. I stuck out my tongue at its retreat.

"Look," Magi gasped.

A branch of the nut tree dipped towards us with two pale buds at its tip. A sweet scent wrapped around us as it bloomed, the petals fell, and the nuts fattened in a span of moments. Two golden hazelnuts dropped from the branch into our outstretched hands.

"Oh, poor Mama." Magi wept as her fingers closed around the nut.

"Hide it, Mags," I said as I shoved my nut deep into one of my pockets. For six years we kept the secret, tended the nut tree, and grew as young girls will. Or rather, I grew more wilful and Magi more beautiful. I grew wilder and Magi gentler. I grew more and more restless, chafing against the rule of our distant but always critical, always watchful father. Magi was the only one who could calm me, her cheer and gentle humour like a beacon of lamplight guiding me safely home through the darkness of my savage and stormy tempers.

Then one day, in our eighteenth year, I slipped through the withy gate to find the garden cast in shadow, quivering with my father's shouts and my sister's tears.

"Who?" Father demanded, holding up the little gold nut as if it were a diseased tooth. "Who gave this to you?"

Magi cast me a despairing glance and Father caught her chin, pulling her gaze back to him.

"Answer me, child!"

"My, I mean, a—" She fumbled for words.

"She found it," I said, as Magi burst out with, "A village boy!"

Father glared at me, although my answer was true enough and hers was ridiculous. What villager had gold to give away? "A boy?" he sneered. In a moment, his rage cooled to icy disdain. "No boy is good enough for you, Magimerismara. Do you think you love him?"

"No!" she cried, truthfully, since he didn't exist.

"And you Tattermog?" His gaze raked over me like the claws of a casually cruel cat. "Have you been trysting with village boys?"

I spread the ragged edges of the three cloaks I wore for warmth and curtseyed to him scornfully. "I've been riding Barleycorn over the crags," I said. "I'm not interested in boys."

"What boy would be interested in you?" He returned his attention to my sister, holding the gold hazelnut up before her tear-stained face. "But you. . ." He flicked the nut into the pool and Magi gasped as one of the silvery fish darted to the surface and gulped it down.

"I see I cannot trust you." Father scowled. "Girls are foolish, weak creatures."

I scowled back, but he paid me no mind.

"I will have to take your soft hearts and keep them safe," he declared.

"T-take our hearts?" Magi stuttered.

"Cobblesnot!" I cried.

"Then you will never fall in love with a man," Father pronounced. In a swirl of shadow, he vanished from the garden to set his plans in motion.

Magi ran to me and held me close.

"I don't see how this can end well," I said, and I urged my sister to leave with me at once, to seek our own fortune out in the world for it couldn't be more dangerous than being subject to the whims of an arrogant, headstrong wizard.

"It's not only loving but living for which we need our hearts," Magi sobbed. "Father is angry, but he'll not let us die."

I waved my spoon at the nut tree, but she shook her head, saying, "He will forget that he said such a terrible thing."

I knew our father was too stubborn to do anything of the sort, but we heard nothing more of it until a month later, when a man looked over the withy gate and hailed me away from the side of the pool.

"Hey, lad!" he called and gave me no more than a shrug when I turned. "Is the wizard here?"

The stranger's sharp nose and straggled, grey-speckled beard made him look like a fox with a half-swallowed hen.

I returned his shrug and said, "Hey yourself, hogsprat. The wizard's in his tower. Go and knock on his door, if you dare, but he doesn't welcome men here."

"He'll welcome me." The man rested his forearm along the top of the gate. "He wants me to make him a heart-shaped locket for a great working."

I raised my brows at him, though I wanted to curse. "You're a goldsmith?"

Some of the swagger left his face. "No," he said. "The wizard has a rare and magical shard of fused glass and tin, and I'm the finest whitesmith in Alatay."

"Mog?" Magi called from the other side of the garden. "Where are you?"

"Be off then, dazwaggle," I told the tinker. "Best not keep a wizard waiting."

"Mog?" My sister rounded a screen of pear tree branches and saw the stranger. "Oh, hello," she said with a small, polite smile.

His face transformed from cocky arrogance to thunderstruck greed.

"Chubblebutt," I muttered, "now he's caught sight of the whole blistering henhouse."

"Tell me your name, Beauty," he said.

Magi's smile dimmed.

"If the wizard finds you know her name, he'll turn you into a snipe," I cautioned.

"You are Beauty." He licked his lips. "The dawning of the sun. The bright gleam of the moon upon still waters. . ."

Colour rushed into Magi's cheeks as she shook her head.

"Poxpellets, a poet," I cursed as Magi clutched my arm. "Don't trifle with wizards, tinker," I called back to him as we hurried from the garden. But the damage was done.

Each morning as he climbed the stairs and each evening as he went back to his room in the village, the tinker peered over the withy gate, hoping for a glimpse of Magi. She avoided him, ignored him, told him kindly that she did not wish to further their acquaintance, told him cruelly that she found him old, ugly, and coarse. It was all one to the tinker. At each rebuff he only smiled knowingly and said, "You'll come to love me, my beauty."

"No," Magi answered each time. "I won't."

"Ah." He would wink, or grin, or leer at her. "In time you will." He ignored me, even when I rapped his fingers with my spoon as he threatened to climb over the gate. He only sucked his knuckles and waggled his eyebrows at my sister.

We went inside and bolted the door. "Why won't he listen?" she cried.

"He doesn't hear what he doesn't like." I scowled. "He thinks he knows best, because he's a man."

"He's a clutbumper," Magi said, which was true enough to make me laugh.

We stayed inside for three days until Father summoned us to his tower. I told Magi we should run away or, better, ride off on Barleycorn.

She shook her head. "He'd find us, Mog. You know he would." She looked down at her pretty dress and soft slippers and added in a whisper, "And then he'd be very angry."

I stuck my spoon in my tangled hair and together, we started up the stairs. The shadows grew denser the higher we climbed.

"Has that tinker gone?" I asked as we came through the door.

Robed and majestic, surrounded by shadows and lit by the glowing coals of his brazier, Father frowned. "Yes," he said, "although I don't see how that concerns you, Tattermog. His work is done." He unfolded a square of white silk and held out a heart that gleamed like a shimmering star. Father turned, and the tin locket caught the light of the coals, glowing blood red and sullen as a bruise. I shivered.

"Come," Father said, beckoning Magi, but she shook her head.

"Mog was born first," she reminded him.

He sighed but nodded and I stepped forward, with Magi close behind me. I looked around the tower room but I could only see one silk-wrapped heart.

"Hold this," he commanded, passing it to me.

"Will it hurt?" Magi asked, but I had no attention for his reply. The metal heart was heavy, far heavier than an empty locket made of glass and tin had any right to be, and it filled me with a dark foreboding. I drew back my arm to fling it out of the window so the hateful thing would smash on the rocks of the mountain. I could not bear the thought of its awful weight touching my sister.

Then my father spoke a word of power and plucked out my heart. I froze for a long, empty moment as that single word echoed inside the cavity of my chest.

"Here is a heart to burn within you," Father said, taking a coal from the brazier. "It shall keep you hale and whole, but it shall never love a man." Father settled the lump of coal into its new home within the cage of my ribs. If I could have moved, I would have shivered from toe to crown as its slow, crackling warmth filled the new silence where my heart had beaten. If I could have spoken, I would have cried out the words that the coal sang into my blood. The creeping, clinging tendrils of the tower's shadows drew back as if my touch offended them, and I grinned. Then my smile fled. Magi stood as still as I had been, her face pinched with pain.

"Broxful addlepate, Father, why did you give her that foul metal?" I demanded.

"Jealous?" he sneered, not sparing me a glance.

"It's cursed, you hootanek!"

"It is ancient and powerful," he said, "as befits a wizard's daughter."

"I'm a wizard's daughter," I shouted. "And now Mags is the cursed child of a pernetticled, durmhangered old fool!"

"Out!" he roared, turning on me. The shadows trembled, but I shook my spoon at him as he raged. "Out you wretched, twisted, little oddsbokken! Back to your rooms, the pair of you. I've wasted enough time on saving you from the folly of your ungrateful, foolish hearts. I have important work—"

Magi shivered and Father shouted. I ignored him and wrapped an arm around my twin to guide her from the tower.

"I'm so cold, Mog," she whispered as we hurried, hand in hand, down the stairs. "Cold and dark, as if I'm filled with shadows. I'm afraid—" She stumbled on a step and let go of me. Despite the darkness, her eyes flashed like light striking a mirror. "I hate you," she said, vicious rage strangling her voice and she no longer sounded like my sister. "I'll destroy you. I'll welcome in death and despair to feast on your bones. There's not enough—"

"Hagstabbit," I cried, caught her hand and gasped. How cold she was!

"Mog," she moaned and flung her arms around me. "What has he done?"

I shook my spoon at the shadows that huddled away from me into the corners of the stairwell. "It looks," I said, "as if Father's made a complete bognobbitted mess of things."

We hurried on, not letting go of each other again. I didn't care about the lump of coal crackling in my chest. I worried over Magi's cursed heart so much that I didn't notice the open withy gate until we were by the pool. Then it was too late.

"Beloved," the tinker cried, flinging himself to his knees before my sister. "I could not leave without you."

"Go away, you nodpot!" I yelled, but he ignored me as usual and grabbed Magi's right hand.

"Come, my love," he said, whiskers twitching as he grinned at her. "Think how happy we'll be, away from these cold mountains." He chaffed her hand between his. "We'll go to Mayminsk and see the king's palace and you'll have a dress as fine as Princess Katiana's and—"

I tugged her left hand. "Back inside, Mags, before—"

She pulled free of us both as the tower's shadow pounced. My sister's eyes flashed white. "Like a princess?" She drew herself up, lip curling into a sneer that Father would have been proud of. "And you think yourself fit to be my prince?" Her voice dripped with disdain, every word sharp-edged to cut and wound, but the feckless tinker only grinned.

"Your prince, your hero, your best beloved. I give you my hand, my—" The shadows drew together with a sound like a thunderclap and Father appeared in the garden.

"Foolish girl!" he shouted at Magi, ignoring my cries that it was all the tinker's delusion. "I took your heart for a reason and now you throw yourself at this unworthy creature."

"Now there will be a reckoning," my sister snarled in that same broken voice she had used on the stairs. "Now there will be a feast for the crows." She flung out her hands as if she meant to tear a hole in the world.

I lunged, but before I could grab her, Father shouted a word of power and transformed her into a fish. With a flick of his hand, he flipped her into the pool.

"Of all the flat-mangled, bursquatted hampats," I shouted over the tinker's anguished cry.

"I will not be threatened and abused in my castle," Father bellowed. "You're both as faithless and foolish as your mother."

I rounded on him with my spoon raised, fury choking my throat, and Father sneered in contempt. "I don't need to change you, Tattermog. You are already a heedless, headstrong beast." He swirled the shadows around him and vanished as abruptly as he'd arrived.

"My love!" The tinker dropped to his knees beside the pool.

"Blathercrack!" I thumped him with my spoon. "Nodbuggler!" I hit him again. "This is all your fault. She didn't love you and now she can't and you still—"

Two fish rose to the surface of the pool. Or rather, one pushed another which thrashed and glared. The tinker, with more sense than I thought he had, snatched the angry fish from the water and threw it onto the bank.

"Pestunipent!" I swore, and it transformed, resuming my sister's shape except for her head.

She gave a burbling cry, turned, and ran through the withy gate.

The tinker leapt to his feet. "Come back, my beautiful glimmering girl," he cried.

I hit him again with my spoon and kicked his shin for good measure, but he only shoved me aside and said, wonderingly, "She called my name."

"We don't even know your name," I said, "and her head—"

"I'll follow her." He clutched at his chest and, for a moment, I felt sorry for him. Surely the curse of the monstrous heart he'd fashioned had poisoned and deluded his own. Then I remembered how he'd leered at my sister before he'd even seen the fused glass and tin that Father had given him to work with. That malevolent shard would have taken root easily in his selfishness.

I slapped him again with my spoon as he cried out, "My Beauty! My love! Though I must search the world, I'll find her again."

"Parsnoodle! Didn't you notice that 'your beauty' now looks like a trout?" Clearly, he hadn't. Still vowing his devotion, he ran after my sister. "Good riddance and bad hunting, you bagpusset!" I shouted after him. How could I restore Magi's head and her heart? I looked around in despair and, from the pool, a fish stared unblinkingly back at me. Was it the same one that had raised my drowning, transformed sister? The same one that had swallowed Magi's golden nut?

I dug through my pockets, finding string and straw, crushed flowers and dry corn cobs, stones and, finally, my mother's gift. I glanced at the nut tree and nodded.

"Brettlespelt," I said, flicking the nut into the air. "Help me, Mother, if you can. The only way Father will give back Magi's head and heart is if I have something he values more."

The fish leapt to catch the nut, then splashed back into the pool. It rose again, opened its mouth and sang, "A box without hinges, key or lid, inside a golden treasure is hid."

"Mama used to sing that to us," I said, frowning to recall the song. "In a stone, a cage, a chest. On a bed though it doesn't rest. Past the mouth that doesn't eat. At the end of the royal street." I grinned at my new piscine friend. "A riddle song and you know the answer, don't you? It must be where he keeps his death."

With a flick of its tail, the little trout leapt from the pool into the rill and slipped like a gleaming arrow through the hole in the garden wall. I tucked my spoon into my tangled hair and whistled for Barleycorn, who met me at the withy gate. Together we clattered down the steps to the village in a headlong, whooping rush to follow a fish, find my sister, and save us both.

Magi was easy to find. Her curse meant she had to stay near water. A deep pool, overhung by spindle-willow, lay a mile beyond the village. My sister had her head in the water when I arrived, but I threw myself off Barleycorn and caught her before she could run off. I held her while she sobbed. There could be no drying her tears, of course. She stared at me with her great, glaucous fishy eyes and shook her head when I asked if she could talk. The light danced and glimmered on her silvery scales. I draped one of my cloaks over her head and told her of my plan.

"Such as it is," I admitted, "but the fish has our golden hazelnuts and perhaps our mother's spirit will help."

Magi gestured to the pool where the silver trout lay in the shallows.

"Then listen," I said, squeezing my sister's hand, "Tiffle and taff, Father may search, and that wretched tinker may hunt, but they won't find we four. We'll follow the river and keep your scales wet, Magi dear. We'll ride Barleycorn and Sweetfish will lead us wherever we must go." I got to my feet and helped my sister stand.

"Does that cold and deadly heart trouble you, Mags?"

In answer, she clung to my hand while the fish sang a sad ballad about a cursed maiden.

"Gallpins," I said and bound our hands together with a strip torn from one of my cloaks before we scrambled onto Barleycorn's back.

It was as well I did, for that terrible metal locket our father had gifted her was a burden of doom that we hauled on every step of that weary journey. It was worse at night when Magi and I were tired and the curse seemed at its strongest. I would jolt from sleep to Barleycorn's bleating to find Magi asleep and the dark thing that rode in her heart looking out through her silvered fish eyes, making her fingers pluck at the knotted cloth binding our hands. I would take my sister in my arms and let the glowing lump of coal inside me warm us both while Sweetfish sang our mother's lullabies.

So we went from the Tangjat Mountains to the sea, following the Otysh River—tripping and slipping, bounding and pounding, over rocks and through forests, past farms and villages, crossing the broad and fertile plains of Alatay where the roads merged to become the King's Way. At last, we reached the great city of Mayminsk, where the river mouth yawned and gushed its tales of travel into the sea.

A mouth that didn't eat at the end of a royal street. . . surely, we were close now?

I tugged the cloak close about Magi's head to hide her from the city folk. They stared enough at two young women riding on a shaggy mountain goat. "Slushputtles!" I shouted at one group of gawkers. "Look any harder and I'll scoop out your eyes with my spoon."

We rode past the docks and the harbour wall, and Barleycorn bounded down a steep set of steps onto a little beach shaped like a shell. High, high above, on a great ridge of black stone, loomed the king's castle. Wide, wide before us stretched the sea, foam-flecked and writhing, and there was Sweetfish, leaping amongst the waves.

"Costering hellican, how do we follow you now?" I called. Sweetfish raised her head from the water and sang a snatch of song. "An' it's ho, ho, the wind'll blow, and the master'll tell ye what ye would know."

It echoed a memory of my mother's voice and I joined in singing the verse. "You must find me an acre of land betwixt the salt water and the sea strand. And plough it up with a devil goat's horn and sow it over with one grain of corn." I grinned at Magi. "We can do that."

I dug a piece of corn out of a pocket and Magi held it while I ground it to dust with my spoon. Then Barleycorn ploughed and Magi sowed and Sweetfish and I sang the song through. Laughter echoed from the harbour wall, but I paid the city folk no mind until a fanfare of trumpets made me turn. Two royal persons, who could only be the prince and princess of Alatay, approached across the sand.

I tightened my grip on Magi's hand and Barleycorn's horn, and we stared as boldly as they did.

"We saw you from the castle," the princess said. Her eyes were as blue as the sea and they sparkled with the same humour that twitched her lips. "And wondered what you did."

Her twin brother took her hand, and they mirrored us, except, of course, that I also held a goat.

"Ashputtle, strumpiggle, gallow and glass," I said. "Our work is done. We have ploughed with a devil goat's horn and sown the acre with one grain of corn."

"Ploughed and sown, a job well done," the princess said. I liked the way her voice sounded as sweet as a high meadow lark but with cool depths like a forest pool.

"Only we wondered why?" The prince's smile faded as he looked from my sister's pretty gown to the tattered cloak that concealed her head. "And, er, who you are?"

"We are Katiana and Zhenya," the princess said. "The king of Alatay is our father."

"We are Tattermog and Magimerismara," I replied. "The wizard of the Tangjat Mountains is our father." That widened their eyes, but I went on. "And this is Barleycorn, and that is Sweetfish, and we are here to lift a curse."

I glanced at Magi, and with a shrug, she unbound her head from the cloak. Matching frowns marred the royal countenances and then the princess stepped forward and took my sister's other hand.

"Cursed?" she said. "Is it painful?" She reached for Magi's cheek and laid her hand against the scales.

"Cursed?" said the prince. "How can we help you?"

I'd not expected their kindness and had to swallow down a sudden surge of heat from the coal inside my chest. "I think that this—" I nodded at a great wave rushing towards the beach, "—is who we must ask for help."

The crowd on the harbour wall shrieked warnings as the prince and princess turned. I feared the wave would crush us but, at the last possible moment, it disappeared into itself, and a man stood on the beach. Well, no, not a man but shaped like one with scales and fins. Waves of kelp fell to his shoulders from beneath a coral crown, and his robes were a swirling froth of pearls and sea foam.

"You have sown and now you will reap," he said in a voice like the pounding of surf onto the rocks. "For what purpose have you called forth King Ichthyic?"

"We have sown for—"

He raised a webbed hand to cut me off and said, gazing at Magi, "What vision of loveliness is this?"

"This poor maiden has been cursed," Prince Zhenya said, laying his hand on the hilt of his sword. "She does not deserve your mockery."

"Mockery?" The Fish King's gills flared. "I do not mock."

Princess Katiana rolled her eyes, making me snort with smothered laughter.

"Bosstockets!" I shouted. "The reaping must be reckoned." The king and the prince bristled, but I went on.

"King Ichthyic, Master of the Sea, the reaping is yours for the doing of a task and the task is no burden to one of your talents. Only follow dear Sweetfish down to the seabed and bring us the chest that lies there."

In less time than it takes to tell, the Fish King returned holding a great iron bound, barnacle-crusted chest. While I cursed and struggled one-handed to break the hasp with my spoon, he wooed my sister. While I swore and reached within the chest to draw out a copper cage, he promised Magi all the riches of the sea. While I cursed again and unlocked the cage to take out a stone, he asked her to marry him. While I pounded my spoon against it to split the stone to free an egg, Mags shook her head, and King Ichthyic scowled while Prince Zhenya smiled.

"All for an egg?" the princess said, kneeling in the sand beside me. "It's a box without hinges, key or lid," I said, "and the golden treasure inside. . ."

I squeezed the egg and, as I'd hoped, a bolt of shadows struck the beach and Father appeared, shaking his fist at me.

"Ungrateful, wretched oddsbokken!" he cried. "Leave my death alone."

"Gladly," I said, "but you must first return our hearts."

"What good will that do you?" He scowled. "Love a man and he will betray you."

"As you betrayed our mother?" I squeezed the egg again and shrugged as he shuddered. "That shard you had the tinker fashion into Magi's heart is cursed," I said. "Take it out and return our hearts, or—" I squeezed a little harder.

"Stop it, you unnatural child. I am your father."

"For all the good that does us," I said, resting the egg on my knee and raising my spoon. I looked him in the eye so he could see that I meant to smash his death to pieces.

"Very well," he cried. He held out his hand, murmured an arcane word, and two red pouches appeared on his palm. "You can have your worthless hearts back but—" He smiled like winter. "—your sister will still have the head of a fish."

Magi gurgled a protest, and I squeezed her hand. King Ichthyic smiled.

"But she must recover if the curse is removed," Princess Katiana protested. Father shrugged.

"You must give her back her head as well," Prince Zhenya said.

Father sneered. "I do not have the strength for more than two great workings," he said, "when my death is being squeezed and threatened."

"Yelpwallop," I swore and pointed my spoon at him. "Then here is my bargain. Restore Magi's own head and her heart. I'll get by without mine and I won't break your death. Agreed?"

"You put my death back in the sea, where it's safe," Father said, "and I agree."

I shoved my spoon in my hair and handed the egg to the princess to hold as Magi helped me to my feet, our hands still bound. Father tucked one scarlet pouch into his robe. Then we drew circles of binding on our foreheads with our left thumbs to show the bargain was set.

"Head or heart first?" Father asked.

I said, "That cursed shard of tin."

He spoke the word of power and swapped the evil replica for Magi's true heart. "Hold this," he said, and passed me the locket. He turned back to Magi and held her fish head as he chanted, his words flowing thickly as if he poured them from a jar of cold honey. Through our bound hands, I felt the magic push against the lingering stain of the curse and Father's folly, seeking her true form.

The mirrored tin heart glinted in my left hand, hot and heavy as a grudge. I looked up into the princess' wide blue eyes. The egg which held Father's death nestled cold and pale in her hands.

"Let me help you," Katiana said. She reached over, her arm brushing mine, and opened the clasp on the side of the locket I nodded my silent agreement, and she tucked the egg inside and snapped it shut.

"Hempsnoggle." The cloth that bound my hand to Magi's unwound.

"Mog!" my sister cried, and Barleycorn bucked and jostled her into the prince's arms.

"What a tragic end to such beauty," the Fish King said and threw himself into the sea.

Father dusted a scattering of scales off his hands and reached for the copper cage. "Now, Tattermog, my death," he said.

"Goes back in the sea, as promised." I flung the cursed heart as hard as I could but, before it hit the water, Sweetfish leapt up and snatched it.

"No!" Father shrieked. He ran towards the sea and, mid-stride, transformed himself into a sleek, black fish that cut through the next wave and swam after Sweetfish. I could only laugh because by tiffle and taff I had sworn Father could search but he would not find us. Well, bad luck and good riddance to him. It was all he deserved, to chase our mother's spirit and try to reclaim his death.

"Thank you," I said, turning to Princess Katiana.

"I was happy to help," she replied, "and you had your hands full." Her smile flashed as she tipped her head to where our siblings stood, locked in an embrace. "As do they."

"You were so brave," Prince Zhenya murmured.

"You were so kind," Magi replied.

"How could I not love you?" they said together.

The princess rolled her eyes, and I snorted as I tried to smother my laughter. She held out her hand and said, "Will you come up to the palace with me? We must let my father know the good news."

"That the wizard of the Tangjat Mountains is gone chasing his own death?"

She flicked another glance towards Magi and the prince and said, "That also, I suppose."

Katiana was right, of course. The real news was that my sister and Prince Zhenya had found a love that would launch a thousand ballads. The king, though he might have worried that Magi was the daughter of his old enemy and sister to a tattered oddsbokken, looked from his son's smitten grin to his daughter's imperiously raised eyebrows and agreed that they should be married as soon as they wished. Which was as soon as the very next day.

We rode to their wedding side-by-side, the princess and I—Katiana on a dainty little white mare, me on Barleycorn—and though we had talked the whole night through, she was strangely silent. The road was long, but not as long as my list of flaws. I could not stop them from jostling for room in my mind.

"Hogswaggle," I swore at last. "Does it bother you that I ride on a shaggy mountain goat and not a beautiful horse?"

She shook her head. "Barleycorn is your friend," she said. "Why should it bother me?"

We rode a little further, but still she was silent.

"Rumdumpling," I cursed. "Does it bother you that I carry this wooden spoon?"

"Your spoon?" A smile twitched her lips. "You can call it that if you like, but I know a wizard's wand when I see one."

She said no more, and we rode until I could no longer bear the silence.

"Scalderpot," I said. "Does it bother you that I'm not as beautiful as my sister?"

"Who says it is so?" Katiana shook her head. "You are more beautiful to me than anyone I've ever met."

"Then what is wrong?" I cried, even as her words fanned the coal within my chest, a flush rising in my cheeks.

"Your heart is gone," she said, dashing tears from her eyes, "and you'll never feel for me as I feel for you."

"Blastgopple," I swore, and tucked my spoon into my hair so I could reach over and take her hand. "I didn't care about my old heart and Father's spell because I never wanted to love a man. I don't need that soggy heart to fall in love with you. . ." I grinned at her and warmed through when she smiled back. "I've done that with a lump of coal."

ABOUT THE AUTHOR

Louise Pieper has a lot of opinions, a lot of black clothes, and a house full of books. Despite these promising qualifications she is allergic to cats and can't bake structurally sound gingerbread so has had to make do with other kinds of work. She lives on Ngunnawal and Ngambri country where she spends a ridiculous amount of time reading and writing. She is an ally, an advocate, and an agitator who never saw a boat she didn't want to rock. You can find out more at www.louisepieper.com.

Love and the Warbeast

J. M. Voss

It was Eroz's day off, and so, when the buzzer rang alerting it that someone was outside, it initially assumed a package had arrived. Unfolding its lithe cybernetic body from the couch, it muted its holotainment feed and sashayed lazily to the door. Not bothering to check the security feed, it flung the door open, leaning on the door frame in a way that it knew looked both sexy and extremely casual. Eroz had spent hours practising the move in the mirror, but would never admit it.

As its apertures adjusted to the bright noon glow, it realised its mistake. This was no courier with a parcel to sign for. Instead, Eroz looked up, and up, at a massive, hulking creature that cast a deep shadow across the doorframe.

It was a Warbeast; a cyborg raised from birth as a living weapon and stone-cold killer. A sleek mountain of angular planes and state-of-the-art electronics, each limb concealing a different deadly weapon, red eyes glowing like points of hellfire beneath a snarling metal mask.

Eroz flinched, wondering which of its past misdeeds had finally caught up to it. Who among its many exes had acquired enough money to hire an entire Warbeast? Ah well. At least it was a classy way to go out.

After a moment, Eroz realised that it wasn't dead yet. The Warbeast was just standing there, looking down at it. The massive claws were sheathed, the myriad of cannons folded away from view. Squinting in the light, Eroz noticed a small pink ribbon on one of the longer head spikes, tied into a neat bow.

Slowly, Eroz relaxed and once again leaned on the doorframe. "Am I correct in guessing that you are a customer?"

The Warbeast inclined her head, just once.

"Ah," Eroz said. "Unfortunately, you've found me on my day off. Now, tomorrow's all booked, but if you would like to come by again the day after that, I should have an opening around—"

"It must be today," the Warbeast interrupted. Her voice was deep and flat, perfectly menacing in a way that made Eroz's circuits thrill with static electricity.

"Oh. Well," Eroz said quickly. "I suppose I could make a little time! I only have an hour though, then I must be off! And I'm charging double!"

The Warbeast inclined her head again. Then, ducking down, she moved into Eroz's loungeroom-slash-office. Scanning the room (literally, the LIDAR grids flashing from her eyes), she sat down carefully on the pink loveseat in the corner. The couch creaked alarmingly under her bulk.

"Yep," Eroz said, flustered, "just sit there, that's fine! If you just chill for a moment, I'll make us some tea, shall I?!"

It didn't wait for an answer, scooting hurriedly into the kitchen. There, it took a moment to just breathe, before putting on the kettle.

While the kettle boiled, it watched the Warbeast through the security feed on its internal HUD. She was fidgeting a little, twisting her armoured talons as though nervous. What a Warbeast had to be nervous about, Eroz had no idea.

Once the tea was done, Eroz steeled itself and reemerged, placing two porcelain mugs on the coffee table. It wasn't actually sure if the Warbeast could consume organic liquids, but either way, the gesture usually came across as polite.

Eroz then sat down opposite, arranging its body into what it hoped looked like a calm and confident pose. "So. . . what brings you to visit a love doctor?"

The Warbeast took a breath. She looked very out of place amongst the chic, modern furniture and tasteful nude paintings. Reaching for a nearby phallic artwork, she picked it up, examining it without really seeing it. Eroz winced as she almost dropped it.

"It's okay!" Eroz prompted. "This is a judgement free space! Whatever it is, trust me, I've heard it before. How about we start with the basics," it went on, when the Warbeast still said nothing. "What's your name?"

"Annihilation," the Warbeast responded, a quiet rumble. "But please call me Anni."

"Okay, Anni," Eroz nodded. "So, if you're here, then I take it you are experiencing some sort of problem. . ?"

"I want to fall in love," Anni blurted out suddenly. "Like how they do in the holovids!" She dipped her head, embarrassed. "I know it probably isn't possible for someone like me. . ."

"Now, that's not true!" Eroz said. "Anyone can find love!"

"Even a creature of war?"

"Oh, yes! There's a market for that, believe me!"

"Truly?" Anni eyed Eroz hopefully.

"Absolutely!" Eroz took out a notebook with a leopard print cover and flipped it open. "I'm happy to play matchmaker, if you'd like? Off the top of my head, I can already think of half a dozen people who would love to meet you. What gender or genders are you primarily interested in dating?"

Anni was silent again for a moment. "Sorry," she said. "I do not know."

"You don't know?" Eroz said. "Okay. Well, who have you had a crush on before? It can be a real person, or someone from the holovids. Again, judgment free space."

"What do you mean by "crush"?" Anni said.

Eroz blinked. "I mean, who have you previously been sexually or romantically attracted to?"

"I don't know," Anni said, servos whining in distress. "I don't think I ever have been. I don't know what attraction means, empirically. That's why I'm here! I want to fall in love!"

". . . Right," Eroz said, and put down the notebook. "My apologies. I misunderstood what your problem was."

"Can you help me?"

"I can certainly try. . ."

"They always look so happy, in the vids," Anni growled miserably. "But I don't even know how to begin to look for what they have! Work is always so busy, and there is no room for love there."

"Well, to start with, you shouldn't hold yourself to the standard of the vids," Eroz said. "Real life isn't anything like that. . ."

It thought for a moment, sucking on the end of its pencil. Then it stood abruptly, moving over to a computer terminal on the wall. "I think you've spent so long in the military, that you've completely missed out on several important formative experiences," it said, typing away. "I think the best place to start is by filling in some of those gaps and seeing what comes of it."

"What do you mean?" Anni said. "What are you doing?"

"I'm cancelling my afternoon plans," Eroz said. "We're going on a date."

#

Eroz and Anni sat at a small, intimate table in the corner of a fancy restaurant on C deck. Beside them, a three-storey glass panel displayed a high-definition loop of a gorgeous ocean promenade, azure waves lapping at the pristine wooden quay. Long-extinct seabirds cried out over the speakers. Occasionally, ports in the ceiling released a puff of cool, salt-scented air.

"Relax," Eroz said, watching as Anni glanced about, her shoulders tense. "If anyone is staring, it's at me, not you."

This wasn't entirely true–the Warbeast was, in fact, drawing eyes. But it wasn't entirely untrue either. Eroz intended to make this first date special, and had consequently gone all out.

It was dressed as a smoking-hot male actor, just like from the vids that Anni liked. Its jawline was razor sharp, hair perfectly coifed, eyes smouldering, chiselled abs outlined beneath a tissue-thin t-shirt. It spoke with a husky voice, accent picked from amongst Sinewave's Top Ten Sexiest in the Orion Sector. It even wore a synthetic rose in its breast pocket. It was the archetypal image of a masculine romantic lead. A single roguish wink from this form could send flocks of male-attracted suitors into fits of dizzying heartache.

Anni, however, was mostly distracted. She kept scanning the area, lasers winking from ports about her person, red eyes flicking this way and that. Eroz could almost see the HUD full of combat data scrolling by.

"No-one is going to attack us here," it said patiently. "This isn't a warzone."

"I know," Anni said. "Habit. Sorry."

"You don't need to apologize. Just remember, this is a date. We're here to talk and get to know each other!"

"Yes, sorry," Anni said again.

A waiter wheeled up to take their order. While he performed professionally, Eroz could tell he was intimidated, his words skipping like a scratched disk.

"I'll have the greenhouse goody bowl, and a mocha latte, please," Eroz said, smiling like a toothpaste commercial. "And for the lady. . ?"

"Three steaks," Anni rumbled. "Rare."

"An ex-ex-ex-ex-excellent choice!" the waiter squeaked. "Would you like a beverage as well?!"

"No, thank you. Wait. Actually, I will get the same thing it's getting."

"Two mocha lattes, got it!"

"You don't HAVE to order a drink," Eroz said to Anni, once the waiter was gone.

"Oh," Anni said. "I. . . everyone else was getting one. I was not sure of the custom."

"Would you like me to send you a file on restaurant etiquette?" Eroz said.

"Yes, please."

"Okay. I also have one here on common first date conversation points. Would you like that too?"

"I would, thank you."

Eroz forwarded the files, and watched Anni scan through them in a couple of seconds.

Nodding to herself, Anni arranged her form into a more relaxed pose, leaning forward on the creaking table, resting her snarling faceplate on the knuckle of her claw. "So," she said in a quiet growl. "Do you. . . have any hobbies?"

Eroz grinned, charmed by her earnestness. It answered her question, and asked her the same, following the script to keep her at ease. She went into enthusiastic detail about her love of high-calibre guns and explosives. Eroz watched her talk, enamoured, wondering how it had ever found her frightening.

Soon, their food arrived. While Eroz deftly forked morsels into its carbon-fuel port, Anni opened a large section of her mask, full of rows upon rows of shearing blades, and placed a steak, whole, inside. She closed the mask again, and a harsh whirring sound emerged, much like a blender. She raised a delicate talon to her mouth and wiped away a small dribble of reddish juice.

They talked some more, trading questions back and forth – personal, but not too personal. Anni told Eroz about her daily life on the warfront, and Eroz tried its best not to look shocked at the casual horrors she described. In turn, Eroz told some of its best funny stories, most of them misadventures in pursuit of love and social standing. Anni did not laugh, but appeared amused nonetheless.

After some time, Eroz paid the bill, and they left the restaurant behind. Eroz offered its hand to Anni, which she shyly took, and they went down to E deck. Here was another popular spot for first dates – a large coolant tank, stylised to resemble a natural lake, with imitation reeds and flocks of whimsical oversized bathtub ducks.

The staff at the paddle boat hire were a little reluctant to let a Warbeast borrow one of their flimsy plastic boats, but were also too scared to tell her no. Folding herself as small as she could, Anni climbed in first, adjusting her weight distribution before Eroz joined her. The paddle boat listed horribly to one side, but it did not capsize. Knee to knee, they paddled out into the middle of the lake.

After chasing ducks for a little while, they came to a stop, floating gently, far from the shore. Above, the ceiling displayed images of a complex, every-changing cloud-filled sky. Below, deep in the crystal-clear coolant, fuel rods glimmered like green stars.

Eroz turned, then, to gaze upon Anni's face. As she looked down, meeting its eyes, Eroz smiled as seductively as it was physically able. "Here's the part where we kiss," it purred. "If you want to."

After a pause, Anni shut off her visuals and leaned down. Eroz rose up to meet her and pecked her once on the faceplate. A small spark fizzled at the point of contact. Anni withdrew again.

"So?" Eroz said after a pause. "What do you think?"

"I'm. . . not sure," Anni said thoughtfully.

"You didn't like it?" Eroz said, trying to hide its disappointment.

"No, it was not bad. I just. . . didn't feel love," Anni said. "Or, at least, nothing out of the ordinary."

"That's okay," Eroz said. "It's quite possible you simply aren't attracted to men. Many people aren't. This form was a guess. We can go for something different next time. "That is, if you would like to try again?" it went on casually.

"Another date?" Anni said. "Sure. While I do not think I felt love yet, this was still fun. I learnt many things. Thank you for taking me out, Eroz."

"You're welcome, Anni," Eroz said. "So. . . when should we meet next?"

#

It was two months later, when Anni was once again free from her military duties. She came to Eroz's house in the early evening, wearing the same pink bow on her head, plus a brand-new shiny arm, replaced after her old one had been blown off.

Eroz was already dressed and waiting, this time as a stunningly beautiful woman. Curvaceous and buxom, with dark, luscious hair to the waist, eyes glinting with wicked mirth, lips full and red. It was clad in rave wear, all straps and latex and reflective panels, just enough concealed to fire the imagination. Opening the door, it chewed on a fingertip, winking at Anni. "I'm SO glad you could make it."

"Nice to see you too, Eroz," Anni responded. She came into the house and sat down on the same couch as last time, causing it to sag even lower than before. "I take it you have already planned out the evening?" Her deep, flat voice was even more menacing than Eroz remembered.

"I certainly have!" Eroz smiled. "A friend of mine is hosting a party this evening. I thought I would bring along you as a plus one."

Anni half rose in alarm. "A party?" she said. "I don't. . . won't my presence disrupt the experience for the other guests?"

"They already know you're coming," Eroz said. "It would actually be ruder of you to dip out!"

Anni sat down again. "Understood," she said. "Then let us go."

"In a minute," Eroz said. "First, I have something to give you. . ."

It disappeared into its expansive walk-in robe, returning shortly with a large bundle of cloth. Dramatically, it unfurled the cloth, revealed a tailored dress, soft grey, with pink and red highlights, perfectly colour-matched with Anni's red eyes and pink bow. There were zips for accessing various combat panels and inbuilt weapons, as well as a multitude of useful pockets.

"What do you think?" Eroz said excitedly. "It should fit you perfectly."

Anni eyed the dress wordlessly for a long moment. "It's beautiful," she whispered. Reverently, she took the dress from Eroz, being very careful not to tear the fabric as she examined it more closely. "Can you help me put it on?"

"Of course!"

Soon, Anni was in the dress. In front of the full-length mirror, she turned back and forth, before spinning around, watching the dress flare out like the blooming petals of a flower. "It's perfect," she said in awe.

Eroz watched her, in awe as well. "It's yours," it said. "Keep it forever. Wear it whenever you want."

"Thank you, Eroz. I will!"

Not long after, they set out to the party. Hosted by a disgustingly rich couple, it was to be the event of the season, a massive, gaudy affair, held across an entire habitation deck. In each room was some new delight or decadence; live music, party games, designer drugs on USBs, canapes and drink, dancing, comedy, shows of light and art. Everyone who was anyone was going to be there, sloshed off their robo-tits.

Eroz once again took Anni's hand as they passed through the front door, bass thundering in their memory wafers. Around them, figures decked out in little but glitter and lingerie gyrated beneath pulsing lights.

Eroz knew many of the guests, and stopped to greet each one, yelling excitedly over the music, introducing Anni as their date to a procession of people. Anni, meanwhile, plucked a flute of white wine from a passing tray, and nursed it carefully, watching the dancing, laughing, intoxicated crowds in fascination.

Together, they explored the party, sampling its delights. Anni tried a little of every dish she came across, taking her time to blend it on the lowest setting. Eroz, meanwhile, accepted drugs from five different people, stowing them away "for later". Briefly, they met one of the hosts, who hugged both Eroz and Anni like she'd always known them, before vanishing again into the crowd.

As they went, Eroz would periodically point out someone across the room and say to Anni, "What do you think? Hot or not?" While Anni was obviously not interested in men who looked like living cologne commercials, Eroz wanted to zero in on what her type was. Emo twinks? Amazonian queens? Hairy dudes with dad bods? Pretty, cottagecore femmes?

Regardless of who Eroz pointed out though, smoke-show or dweeb, Anni's response was always the same: "I don't know. They look nice."

"Even in that shirt?" Eroz countered peevishly.

Anni shrugged again. "The khaki reminds me of my recharge box back at HQ."

Eventually, the two of them came to a quieter room, where the music played a little muted, and the lights were dim. There, with no one else around, Eroz showed Anni how to dance. Hands lightly brushing her body, it guided her to move with the music, laughing as Anni's initial uncertainty transmuted into confidence and enjoyment, her natural athleticism translating well into ability.

Soon, they were dancing, faster and faster. Others came in to watch the spectacle, and then to join them, packing the room in writhing bodies. As the crowd reached a critical mass, Eroz, laughing, dragged Anni away again, into the sudden stillness and quiet of an empty room.

Eroz collapsed onto a soft, air-filled couch, shaped like a cloud. "Join me!" it said, patting the seat beside it.

Anni carefully did so, and Eroz wriggled over to sit in her lap. Looking up, it met Anni's eyes, and unleashed a playful grin, wicked enough to set even the most stoic of hearts a-thunder. Leaning in slowly, it whispered directly into Anni's audio-processor: "If you want to kiss me again, you can."

Anni was silent for a long moment. Then, again, she slowly bent down. Their faces met briefly, and again, a single spark flared.

Eroz held its breath as Anni pulled away. "Feel anything?" Eroz said, with bated breath.

But Anni sighed. "I'm sorry," she said. She sounded upset.

"Nothing, then?" Eroz fought to not let its dismay show. "That's okay! Sometimes it takes a while. Months. Years even!"

"No, I should have felt something by now!" Anni growled. "You're beautiful. I can see that much. You were last time as well. Anyone other than me would be smitten. They ARE smitten. I've seen the way they all look at you here. Everyone is in love with you, except for me."

"It's fine," Eroz said, "you can't force these things! Maybe, I'm just not your type? Or maybe, you've put too much pressure on yourself? If you just give yourself more time—"

"I am sick of waiting!" Anni snarled suddenly – and long blades emerged from her hands, savagely impaling the couch. Eroz fell silent, its mouth ajar. With a hiss of air, the couch deflated, collapsing into itself.

Anni retracted her blades with a metallic SNICK, and stood abruptly. "I'm sorry. I should go. I am a machine of war. I am not built for love."

"Wait!" Eroz called—but it was too late. The Warbeast had vanished, disappearing amidst the strobing lights of the dancefloor.

#

Three months passed, and Anni did not return. Every day, Eroz thought of her, wondering whether she'd ever come back. Every day, it regretted the things it had said, and not said, to her.

Then, on its first day off in the fourth month, Eroz heard a knock on the door. Trying not to hope, it opened the security feed—and there she was, standing on the doorstep, fidgeting with her own claws. She was wearing the grey dress, singed and torn in several places.

Telling itself to stay cool, Eroz opened the door, and wordlessly held it wide. Anni came in and sat again on the pink couch in the corner.

"I'm sorry," she said after a moment. "For ruining the dress you gave me. And for everything else."

"You apologise too much," Eroz said. "The dress was made to be worn. And everything else was my fault."

"No," Anni said. "I lost my temper. I scared you. That's not what I wanted."

"Your emotional reaction was totally reasonable," Eroz said. "I heaped far too many expectations on you, far too quickly. You were right to be mad. I should have known better. In fact I. . . I have analysed the data from our dates, and have come to the conclusion that you might be ace."

"What?" Anni said. "What does that mean?"

"I am someone who falls in love easily," Eroz said. "I sometimes forget that not everyone is like that. I get carried away, fall in love every other week with someone new. Meanwhile, you told me that you'd never even had a crush before. But Anni—and I should have thought to say this sooner—there's nothing wrong with that! Many people are the same as you. Sometimes, they'll take years to fall in love with someone. Decades! Or sometimes, they never fall in love at all."

"Never?" Anni said glumly.

"Never," Eroz said. "But again, there's nothing wrong with that."

"But," Anni said, "I WANT to fall in love. I want to be happy!"

"You don't need romantic love to be happy," Eroz said. "In fact, many are happier without it!"

Anni blinked. "Oh? So, what should I do, then?"

"Whatever you want!" Eroz spread its arms dramatically. "Whatever you enjoy, and whatever brings you peace. And while you do those things that make you happy, one day, love may show up. Or it might not. But either way, you'll be content."

"In other words, I should just give up?" Anni sighed. "I knew you couldn't help me. . ."

"No!" Eroz said, "you're not listening! Look," it stood up, "how about I show you instead?"

"Show me what?"

"Platonic love," Eroz said. "C'mon. Get up. We're going out on one last date. . ."

#

This time, Eroz did not dress up, wearing only its bare cybernetics and personality - plus a cute crop-top that complemented its RGB frame lighting.

This time, it did not take Anni's hand, but raced her instead, to the games arcade on G deck.

Anni won by a significant margin, watching Eroz come puffing around the corner with amusement in her red eye points. "Keep up," she said, as it dramatically collapsed to the floor at her feet.

In the arcade, Eroz let Anni choose which game to play first. She picked an alien shooter, and promptly obliterated the previous high score. After that, they played a basketball hoop scoring game, which Anni also dominated at.

"Cheater!" Eroz scolded her, when she admitted to using a parabola tracing algorithm.

Next, they played a dance game, which Eroz was finally able to win – although Anni was catching up with alarming speed. "At this rate, you'll get the high score in every damn game in the arcade," Eroz said, impressed.

They played a few more, before they went out to get lunch. They did not go to a restaurant, but a grungy hole in the wall, selling cheap, greasy food, that was absolutely delicious. Eroz laughed as Anni opened her face plate and blended an entire basket of hot wings, bones and all. Around them, people were staring – but neither cared.

Finally, they went together to try out a new stargazing experience that had just opened on H deck. After waiting in line for a long time, they were shuffled into a small cubicle, which extended slowly out of the side of the space station.

The lights went out, and the walls and floor of the cube became transparent. Suddenly, they were standing in open space. Stars surrounded them, red and blue, white and gold, above, below, and reflected behind in the mirror-like walls of the station. At a touch, constellations were revealed, worlds and systems, trade routes and warzones, all so tiny from here, and yet unimaginably vast.

They were allowed five minutes, before the staff kicked them out to make way for the next group. Silent, humbled by the sight of the galaxy laid out before them, they moved away from the attraction.

"So," Eroz said eventually, as they slowly headed back towards its home. "Do you understand my point yet? About platonic love?"

"Maybe," Anni said quietly. "I think I'm beginning to, anyway. Today has been fun. All of the dates were."

"I'm glad to hear it," Eroz said. "Although with friends, it's called hanging out. Or catching up. This was a catch-up, not a date."

"So," Anni said, eyeing Eroz, "you're not annoyed at me, then? For not falling in love with you?"

"No! No, of course not!" Eroz said. "To me, love comes cheaply. It's really no big deal. I'll be in love with someone else by tomorrow. In the meantime, I'd much rather have you here as a friend."

Anni nodded. The, abruptly, she brightened.

"Oh! I forgot! I had a new faceplate installed. The old one was far too serious. I could not even smile with it—and you're smiling at me all the time. I wanted to be able to return the gesture."

"You did that, for me?" Eroz said.

"Yes."

"Hah. Then you do get it, Anni. That's love right there."

Anni blinked. Then, with a slight grating noise, her face mask altered its shape, so that she was smiling at Eroz. "I'll accept that," she said.

ABOUT THE AUTHOR

J.M. Voss is an award-winning science-fiction author based in Naarm/Melbourne. She is on the ace spectrum, and GNC, which means she likes garlic bread, and expanding the frontiers of gender through a range of "unladylike" interests and fashion choices. Strangely, many of her characters turn out the same. Find her on Facebook, Bluesky, or check out her website for more information on upcoming projects.

The Amethyst Isles

Frank Lee Howe

Sir Dane of Crestwood looked out to sea, letting his shoulder length brown hair catch in the sea breeze. He'd always assumed he'd be precisely the kind of person who'd suffer seasickness, but he found he immediately took to this mode of transport with surprising tranquillity. The smell of the salty brine, the crispness of the air, the rocking of the waves, and the flapping of the sails; it all appealed to him. He'd been discovering quite a few new things about himself of late.

Chief amongst which was the discovery that he was what they called one of the 'changelings'. Children of the faerie folk, touched by magic whilst still in the bellies of their parents. Changelings were indistinguishable from other children, only exhibiting certain qualities and differences that separated them. The old tales spoke of the faerie folk swapping out infants in the middle of the night with their own kind but in an age of enlightenment, scholars likened them to a cuckoo bird who smuggled their eggs into the nest of other birds to trick them into raising their offspring.

Unlike the cuckoo, the changelings were celebrated. It was considered a great blessing to have been chosen to raise one. Then there were the honours bestowed onto the changelings themselves. Every four months there was a great celebration for them in the kingdom, where they were gathered for a banquet and put on a parade that ran from the capital square to the docks where the ship, *The Periwing,* would take them across the Slender Sea to their true home, the Amethyst Isles, to be reunited with their kin.

Typically, those who discovered the signs were younger than Sir Dane. It had taken him some years to realise he was one of them, having been so focused on his training. He was close to twenty-two before he became aware. At least beyond the shadow of doubt. Those who had joined him in the parade were all teenagers. The oldest of which was a month or so shy of nineteen and the youngest was fourteen. Boys who realised they had affections for other boys and girls being as fond of other girls was supposed to be the first sign of being a changeling. As both a young man in his twenties and a knight, he was the most prominent of the selection to have been honoured with the journey to their real homeland where they would discover all the other things that made them different.

"You're so rarely found inside," Kevin said. An elegant young man, he bore near white, blond hair and a beauty spot upon his cheek. If the elves of old stories had been real, he might have been mistaken for one. The second oldest of the batch of changelings aboard, he had a habit of gravitating towards Sir Dane. "Always out on deck."

Sir Dane smiled. "What is the point of travelling by sea if you do it inside, surrounded by wooden planks and beams?" he retorted. "You can surround yourself in such structures on land. But this. . ." he pointed out across the waves. "This, you do not see elsewhere. This great expanse of blue between sand and soil is far too exotic an experience to cower under low ceilings in swinging lantern light."

Kevin smiled. "It *is* beautiful. Though some of our fellow changelings have not taken well to traversing it."

"It is not for everyone, I've always heard. But now that I'm here, I find it breathtaking."

Kevin nodded. "Everyone speculates about you. You're something of a guest of honour amongst our number."

"Because I'm the oldest?"

Kevin nodded.

"Yet, you're not so far behind."

"Yes, but I wilfully dragged my feet. I think I always knew I was this way. I just didn't say anything."

Sir Dane looked to him in surprise. "You delayed this honour?"

Kevin shrugged. "I had seen the parade so many times and wanted to be a part of it. By delaying my revelation, I got to enjoy the pageantry of it more times than most."

"It had never occurred to me to attend," Sir Dane admitted. "I never really put that much thought into it. I saw from afar, but I was so focused on becoming the knight I believed I should be for my king. Never realising that I would carry my honour across the sea and be a knight of the Amethyst Isles instead."

"You must be quite the fighter to have been so focused on your training, you paid no attention to your more personal desires."

Sir Dane nodded as he reflected on it. "The girls were always quite fond of me. It just never seemed to occur to me to do what the other boys did when it came to them. I would talk and they of course listened as I did in return, but I just never ended up steering the talk to whatever sweet nothings boys tell girls to be granted a hand beneath their garments. I enjoyed their company but lacked the predatory nature of other boys. Besides which, I was never really sure what was to be gained from doing any of those things. I suppose that should have been a bit of a clue."

Kevin smiled and shook his head. He looked down to the waves trickling against the wooden hull. "I knew I felt about boys, the way other boys felt about girls, the moment they started fondly talking about them. They spoke of them the way I felt about *them* instead. I could have announced myself and joined others on this journey *years* ago, but I suppose I was simply afraid to leave my mother behind. We were always so close."

"It wasn't easy to leave *my* friends and family behind. But this is the way of things. We are headed to our true home. Where we belong. I shall miss my old life, but to carve my way through the waves of the Slender Sea to face my destiny thrills me endlessly."

"So, when did you know?" Kevin asked, sliding his hands along the copper railing as he moved closer. "For it to happen so late, what was the moment?"

"The last Summer Tourney. Did you attend?"

Kevin shook his head.

"Had you revealed your true self, you would have had honoured seats."

"Not really my sort of thing," Kevin said, scrunching his nose. "Not that I don't admire those who participate." He gave a warm smile as the sea breeze upswept his silky hair. "Did you do well?"

"Typically, I always do. But I found myself a little distracted this last tourney."

"Oh?" Kevin sang, with curious delight. "Who was he?"

"Sir Bradley of Melbany. An absolute stallion of a man. A proud posture, strong jaw, and hair like spun hay. Always some sly jape on the tip of his tongue. The women loved him. When the two of us entered the grounds there wasn't a sitting woman or girl in the pavilion or stands. Our fight wasn't the last event, but it was the one everyone was waiting for." Sir Dane leaned on the railing and smiled nostalgically. "It was a good combat, and I at least went the distance. But in the end, he had me off my feet, straddled over my belly as I lay on the ground facing up. He looked down on me with his eyes as blue as the clear sky behind him and smiled his handsome smile. The crowd was cheering as he rested upon me, catching his breath from the fight. What were his precise words, again? Something like '*oh well,* 'he said, patting me on the chest plate. *'Can't sit around on you all day, unfortunately. Must get showered in flowers from the maids, ladies, and princesses.'*" He sank his head with a reflective smile. "He pushed himself up off me and went and did just that. But I continued to lay there on that thin layer of sand, staring up at the great pale arches in the sky that sailors say circle the world. I lay there thinking about what it might be like if he *had* actually had the time to sit atop me, as he had, all day. It had been merely a jape. A friendly bit of banter to amuse a humiliated opponent to soften the edge of defeat. But the image lingered, and I welcomed it. I wanted it. I desired it. I pondered on it so long that my squire came to fetch me, thinking I'd been concussed. He pulled me up and walked me off the tourney grounds and to my tent."

Kevin grinned enthusiastically at the story. "Quite an awakening," he said, before his smile slipped into a sympathetic pout. "As Sir Bradly hasn't joined us on this voyage, I'm guessing his words truly were nothing more than jest."

Sir Dane nodded with disappointment. "Unfortunately, so. But the land of our faerie folk forebears awaits. There we shall be rewarded with the affections of those who love as we do. There, in the promised land of the Amethyst Isles where the worldly delights we crave are offered freely. A rich land of—"

"Yes, we've all been told of it. But there's still some of our trip left. We could wait as instructed, or. . ." Kevin looked around. "It seems a big enough ship to house some quiet and forgotten corners that are rarely visited. We could find somewhere and. . ." he raised his eyebrows and placed a hand over Sir Dane's. "I'm no Sir Bradley of Melbany, by the sound of it, but I *do* have time to do what he merely japed about."

Sir Dane pulled his head back, caught off guard but smiled at the invitation.

\#

Days later, a bell rang and the honoured guests were summoned to deck. Making their way to the bow of the ship, the seven who had been selected for the journey took their first look at the enchanted land from which they truly came. An archipelago with one large island surrounded by smaller ones. All of which boasted purple flowers that crowned the base of rocky inclines beyond the beach of each island into incomplete mountains that occupied the vast majority of the land. It was a beautiful and mysterious sight.

"How unusual," Kevin said, standing by Sir Dane's side. He'd barely left it since they paired off.

The other five were young teenagers, excited and all staring out across the remaining water. They had all heard the stories growing up. It was a tropical paradise within natural mountainous walls that obscured the magical wonderland within from the outside. For decades, those celebrated in the streets before leaving for this place had come, reuniting with all who had come before them and awaiting the tri-annual delivery of more of their kind.

The ship anchored as the seven were directed towards a boat to be rowed to shore. As Sir Dane climbed over the railing to scale down the scramble net, he instinctively reached for his scabbard to steady his sword. Finding nothing there, he smiled at his own folly. Told he'd need no armour or weapons where he was going, he had surrendered them to his parents to remember him by. He had made them proud as a knight of the realm and served the kingdom, in tourneys and other honours. But he felt a little naked without the tools of everything he'd aspired to become.

He climbed into the boat and helped the others as the large-bellied captain waved them off. The crewman brought them ashore and quickly left. It had always been said that the Amethyst Isles were no place for humans who were untouched by the faerie folk, and they were not permitted to set foot ashore. The seven looked in wonder at their surroundings as the crewmen rowed their boat back to the ship.

Strange birds with long curved beaks flew back and forth between the islands. From afar, the greyish brown rocky inclines had made the islands look like a collection of giant felled tree trunks with jagged ridges. The seven along the beach towards a low point in the rising rock, down the coast. From behind it, the spires of what appeared to be a crystal palace reached above the rocks, reflecting the sunlight into many colours. They all smiled with wonder at the sight of it.

"No doubt, a beautiful and exotic place dwells within these natural walls," Sir Dane said.

Kevin slid his fingers into Sir Dane's hand and grasped it. "So, this is home."

"And long has it waited for your return," an unknown voice said from behind the group.

They all turned around and found standing on the sand an elegant figure. It was a man, at least in shape. His skin was glossy and pearlescent, cream coloured with faint hints of purple and blue that shifted in the light. He wore a short garment of rich green, littered with tiny sparkling particles, existing within the thread. His head was hairless with ridges from his cheeks and hairless eyebrows that led to a point high on the back of his head. His eyes were yellow in hue.

"That is Castle Glarromore, where the regents rule these Amethyst Isles. You shall be welcomed guests there, soon enough." He smiled at their confused faces. His feet barely scrunched the sand beneath them., as he paced about them, far lighter than he appeared. "My name is Sedo, and I have come to welcome you to these shores. Walk with me and tell me of your lives so far, amongst the humans." He gestured for them to continue down the coast.

On the walk, Sir Dane spoke of his life as a young knight, distinguished in tourneys and for aiding the king's men in apprehending bandits and rebels. Kevin spoke of his father, a woodworker to whom he was apprentice. The next oldest, a girl named Larissa, had barely begun serving on a small coastal fishing ship, at only fifteen. The others had yet to find or learn their skills, a few taking jobs and tasks suited to those in their early teens but with little else to share, being still so young. They all told their short tales of their youthful lives so far, as Sedo walked them along the beach.

They reached a stone tunnel protruding from the natural rock wall. Inside, two more like Sedo stood waiting. They each opened a side of a two-door entrance and where Sir Dane had expected a vista of some wonderful new faerie kingdom, there was instead a small dining hall. Platters of fruit and fish filled a long table with goblets of frosted twisted glass filled with ale. The room was carved into the rock, polished smooth and glossy.

"Come and dine with us," Sedo said. "This is your homecoming, and what better way to start than with a meal in your honour."

"Is no one else joining us?" Larissa asked.

"This meal is all about getting to know you better as you relax, so that we might find the right places for you here. There will be plenty of time to meet your brothers and sisters of these Isles."

Sir Dane sat and drank and ate the exquisite food. There was talk and laughter, then there was yawning and tired eyes.

#

Sir Dane woke up in little more than a loincloth, and an abundance of chains. Some growling abrasive voice was yelling at him. "Get up," he realised they were saying. When he looked about, he was in a coarse stone room, long and divided by walls of iron bars.

"What's this?" he asked, looking up to the creature leaning over him.

A large stocky figure was helping him up with a less than gentle hand. Reptilian, it had the skin of a lizard, with short stocky legs, and long arms. It was as if a gecko was walking upright and had grown a large pot belly, then put on iron pauldrons, cuffs, and a chest piece of loose pieces linked together by leather straps.

"Welcome home, *changeling*," he mocked. There were others like him who laughed.

Other humans were sitting on benches in other sections separated by iron bars that made barriers between natural stone pillars and other formations. He was in a dungeon of some kind. The other humans all had terrible injuries. Missing ears, noses, arms, legs, with scars, eyepatches, bandages, and slings. An old man was in the next cell. His grey beard was thick and missing a section where a broad scar ran down his cheek.

"How did I end up *here*?" Sir Dane demanded, confused and outraged. "What happened?"

"You were lied to by your king," the old man said. "Then you were poisoned by the monstrous races that dwell here. The masters who are beautiful to the eyes but beastly in spirit, and these lizard folk who are beastly in appearance and devoid of anything worth describing in spirit."

"Do not make me strip your back of more skin," the lizard man in Sir Dane's cell warned him, holding up a whip with five tails.

The grey-bearded man gave a look of bitter defiance.

"There's been some mistake, I am an honoured guest of. . ." Sir Dane began to protest, but his captors laughed.

"We are not honoured guests," the old man said. "We are the refuse, cast away by a kingdom that openly celebrates our kind only to ensnare us, parade us, and then push us onto ships. Slaves, sold to placate a neighbouring force and purchase peace and prosperity with cruel foreigners."

Sir Dane was still confused. "But what of the faerie folk? Are we not changelings?" he asked, fuelling further laughter from his monstrous captors.

"A clever ruse to ensure compliance," a woman in the cell on the other side of Sir Dane's said. She bore an eyepatch and many scars, sporting short black hair. "To rid the kingdom of *undesirables*, it was King Leonard the second who brokered a deal with these... people. He hated our kind as did many of his day. His father, Leonard the first, had openly persecuted our kind as deviants but times changed, and many people were against it. So, Prince Lenny the second came up with a rather elegant solution to routinely rid his father's kingdom of our kind. Concocting this whole faerie folk myth. On one hand it made the more ignorant commoners less abusive, but this is the reward for being different."

"Your first fight is tomorrow," the large lizard man said, locking the cage from the outside. "Be ready."

"Fight?" Sir Dane asked, still digesting the great lie he'd believe in his whole life.

"We're pit fighters in here. All soldiers, knights, town guards, militiamen, and mercenaries back home," the old man said. "They make us fight each other, others like the guards in here, and also beasts they underfeed."

"Everyone else is a slave of labour best suited to whatever task they were most closely trained in," the woman explained.

Sir Dane looked to the ground, realising that Kevin was likely put to the task of building. It made him grind his teeth in anger. Thinking of his parents, so proud of him and honoured to have raised one of the faerie folk. His *actual* parents. Generations of people like himself sent to this place with joy in their heart, proud and honoured as they marched to their doom, separated from their real families. He remembered seeing the current king, the king that had knighted him, presiding over the parade to honour his departure. He had been secretly despising him in disgust, mocking him with such a display as he sent him off into thraldom by isles of monsters.

"These fights. . ." he asked, looking at neither of his neighbours but addressing them both. "Do they arm us?"

"Of course," the woman said.

Sir Dane bitterly grinned, as a deep fury bubbled within. "Then that will be their first mistake."

#

The time to enter his first fight came and Sir Dane obeyed instructions from the cells to the arena ramp. It was not until a portcullis was lowered behind him that he was given access to a sword and shield.

"Prove yourself, human," the lizard-like creature behind the bars said.

"What?" Sir Dane asked, furrowing his brow.

"Prove yourself."

Sir Dane shook his head and looked to the three fighters accompanying him, feigning confusion. He then looked to the guard and took a few steps back towards the bars while the forward cage door was lifted. "No, I didn't catch that, sorry."

"I said prove yourself, human," the guard barked in annoyance, leaning into the bars as Sir Dane walked up to them. "Something wrong with your ears?"

Sir Dane pulled the guard's arm through the bars and drove his sword deep under his armpit into the side of his chest. The guard gasped shocked, unable to call out for aid. "Is that the sort of proof you were after?" he asked, twisting the sword to open the wound before pulling it out. He looked the reptilian guard in his large, bulging eyes as the life rushed out of him. "One down, the rest to go."

Sir Dane stormed out into the arena, carried by the rush of what he had done. His companions were all stunned but wasted no time in following him. No plan, no biding his time. He would not agree to a single whole day of this life he'd been sentenced to. "Death to the reptiles, death to the masters, and death to King Leonard the fifth."

His companions excitedly repeated his words.

"The fight begins now," he declared.

Hearing the guards reopen the portcullis Sir Dane smiled, knowing more guards were coming for him. Captives rushed from the other side of the arena to meet them in battle for the amusement of the crowd high above in the stands, and those on a balcony of the resplendent crystal palace that looked down over the arena from all its shimmering glory as colours danced about its twisting edges. Sir Dane walked with open arms then stopped and pointed his sword behind him to the ramp from which he and his companion's had come. Two reptilian guards were rushing up, awkwardly. Their bodies incapable of moving with both haste *and* elegance.

Sir Dane looked back to his proposed opponents, pitched against their fellow thralls. "You can fight us, or you can join us and fight *them*. Your enemy. Our enemy. Today we fight for our freedom. There are weapons in your hands, and you have friends with weapons in theirs. Let us take down this place so that we may return home to punish those who sent us into this torment."

A look of uncertainty washed over the other group, followed by one of desire. A stir of rebellion, revolution, and revenge. Two groups of four became a single group of eight focused on the two pursuing guards and a third, lagging behind as he stopped to assess the situation. The first two were swarmed, surrounded, and slaughtered by the armed thralls, plunging their blades deep into their leathery, scaly flesh.

"Quick," Sir Dane yelled, ignoring the instinct to gloat or raise his arms in triumph to the confused crowd. He ran after the third guard who panicked and turned around, calling for more guards. "Stop him before he shuts the gate."

The eight sprinted and tackled the guard to the ground, blades piercing him many times as he squirmed beneath his attackers, spilling his blood and innards down the ramp. Entering the armoury, they took every weapon and shield off the walls and brought them into the dungeon. Soon more guards were surprised and slaughtered while prisoners were freed and armed, taking the sparse armour provided for the fights and even the ill-fitting armour off the dead guards who'd tormented them.

"So, what's the plan now?" the old, grey-bearded soldier asked.

Sir Dane shrugged. "I don't know, but I didn't spend my life training to fight for the amusement of slavers."

"Right. . . well, I wish I'd had *your* spirit when I arrived. Some planning would have been good, but the wheels are turning and this cart's already moving . . . There'll be more guards soon, probably assuming we want to make our way to the dungeon on the other side of the arena to free the other fighters."

"A correct assumption, to their credit," Sir Dane agreed. "How hard is that going to be?"

The old man pondered a moment and grinned. "Doesn't seem like you were out there long enough to notice, but there's more than two ramps into the arena. The next one on the way is for the beasts."

A devious grin crept across Sir Dane's face.

#

The growing group of armed prisoners pushed through the back tunnels of the arena, fighting through more lizard guards. Their captors, while robust and skilled, were unprepared for such an event, never expecting so rash and wild a rebellion. Their spears were not ideal for fighting in such closed quarters and when met by the arena weapons of the bitter captives, more reptilian blood was spilled than human.

At the old man's suggestion, those with shields formed a defensive line at the front, blocking the way they'd come. With the pulling of levers, the cages of the various beasts held in captivity were released. Given the choice of gnashing their teeth and claws against united shields and blades or free passage towards those who'd mistreated and starved them, they opted for a large group of guards running down the corridor. The menagerie of exotic beasts bounded on all fours to their cruel captors.

Though some strayed, smelling the abundance of unwashed, sweaty slave flesh spattered with the blood of guards whose corpses lay strewn behind them, these were beasts trained and instinctually accustomed to chasing their prey. The pursuit of the guards was too tempting an offer to ignore. They pushed the guards back in their attack and took many with them before succumbing to the guards' spears.

When the last beast fell, the escaped warriors pushed ahead and completed their carnage by barging their shields into the lizard men. Wounded, surprised, and with little room to manoeuvre, the guards did not perform so well in the fight.

"Guarding us behind cages, they've grown lazy and complacent." The woman with the eyepatch observed. "Fools relying on circumstance to dominate our will."

Tucking their swords and axes into their armour they all gathered the guards' spears and hurled them into those guarding the prisoners at the other end. The slaves had also accepted circumstance until they were reminded of what could be achieved in numbers.

"Arriving to find out you were so despised and condemned by your king, distracted you," Sir Dane said, rallying the freed fighters. "You have shown this day, you are still the vital weapon wielders you always were, and better yet, you've been hardened by violent captivity." All present cheered with fury.

#

For days they held and controlled the arena tunnels. The kitchen slaves continued to feed them, especially with the fresh flesh of the slain fighting beasts. The masters sent in more and more of their lizard guards in attempts to reclaim the inside of the arena but soon saw the folly in it. All the security they had implemented into housing fighting slaves had inadvertently made it a stronghold. A fortress of tunnels, ill fitted for spearmen to breach. One dangerously close to the regents' resplendent palace, which they could not afford to leave under-guarded, nor the other working slaves as inspiring word of the occupying uprising inevitably spread.

Sedo was sent to parlay with them in the end. "Quite the accomplishment," he admitted, standing surrounded in one of the arena's tunnels. "Generations have gone by and none have quite roused the thralls as you have done. But what do you mean to do here? You cannot hold this place forever."

"To evade recapture, we are willing to die," Sir Dane said. "And also, to free our brothers and sisters. Are you willing to die to keep them?"

"And if you free them?" Sedo asked. "Then what? Where will you go? Do you imagine the king who sold you into slavery will welcome you back with open arms?"

"That's really *our* problem. The question is whether you want us to become *his* problem or stay here and remain yours. We can either kill your regent, or you can let us go and we'll kill ours, instead. Because we'll fight to the last man to achieve either goal."

The other thralls cheered.

Sedo pulled back nervously. "Ours will not want to lose an entire class of servants."

"Then it is perhaps time you repurposed the reptile guards, as their ability to quell rebellion has proven underwhelming."

"What if we just let *you* go. Your band of rebels. We could give you a small ship and send you back."

Sir Dane's contemplative silence concerned his fellow rebels. "You have to know that I wouldn't settle for that. We would return."

"Once you've dealt with your own king and his army?" Sedo said, with an opportune look on his face. "In the gambling spirit of the place under which we now stand, I'll take that wager. If you succeed and what's left of you return, we shall face whatever challenge that may present, *if* and when that time ever comes. But I openly send you, with the expectation that you likely won't return."

"Then I make one demand. In addition to all who served within this arena, you at least return to us those with whom I arrived. It is one thing to turn my back on those trapped here already, but I cannot have those, with whom I came, left behind."

"I will have to see what I can do," Sedo said, backing away.

"Then hurry," Sir Dane suggested. "For when we run out of food, we will turn to the many guards we have slaughtered, and when that flesh is gone, we shall wonder what manner of light flesh sits beneath those resplendent shells of yours. Something akin to crab meat and lobster, I would guess."

Sedo looked both disgusted and fearful, though he tried his best to conceal it. A ruse undermined by his quick pace out of the tunnels.

When the native of the enthralling kingdom left, the other pit fighters surrounded Sir Dane and demanded explanation for agreeing to Sedo's terms.

"Haste has served us well so far, but from this time forward we must plan things carefully," Sir Dane assured them. "Sedo is correct in assuming we would fall against the knights and soldiers of Leonard the Fifth. Not only that, but an open rebellion back home would bring doom down upon our kind and when whatever peace fails between this kingdom and our own, they will be blamed for it. It would return us to a time of Leonard the First. A time well buried by this lie we have suffered for generations. When we return, it must be done in secret. We shall recruit our countrymen and women in subtler means. Our brothers and sisters, and the families of those who lost their children to this place, not yet knowing they should be grieved for. We shall raise rebellion properly. We shall expose and bring down that tyrant, Leonard the fifth. Leonard the last. Then we shall return in great numbers and make war with these Amethyst Isles until everyone like us is free."

Nods and mumblings became chatter and fist shaking. Soon there was a united hum of approval and purpose. "Death to King Leonard," they began chanting and Sir Dane smiled proudly, joining them.

#

The masters of the archipelago kingdom were at least true to their agreement, thinking it would be the last they would see of the rebels. It was a bitter sacrifice for the rebels to make. World would spread that the uprising had only served those who fought. That they left the rest behind would crush the spirit of the remaining enthralled. But they vowed to each other, they would one day return for them.

Manned by escaped slaves, the ship sailed back across the Slender Sea and Sir Dane stood at the bow of the ship, taking in the crisp sea breeze with Kevin once more by his side. A new task lay ahead of them. They would have to find somewhere secret to dock and infiltrate their own kingdom like spies from another.

It was a lucrative lie they had been fed, and one ingrained over much time. It would not be easy to convince their brothers and sisters to abandon it. Subtlety and secrecy were required. As well as time and patience. But they would be back for the rest.

For now, they knew they sailed towards a new future. One they would face and shape together.

ABOUT THE AUTHOR

Frank Lee Howe enjoys writing short stories, especially as an excuse to deconstruct tropes in popular media. Typically working in contemporary fiction, occasionally dabbling in speculative. He has been involved in other forms of media, but writing is his favourite format, loving the art of conversation - especially if he's controlling both sides of it.

A proud ally who lives on Cammeraygal country.

He loves dogs, will tolerate cats, and has yet to meet a horse he didn't get along with.

https://frankleehowe.wordpress.com/

Polish

Kaaron Warren

The car was smooth, air-conditioned, and completely wrong.

"We should be suffering," I said to Callie.

She was driving, sucking barley suger, silent.

"We should be hot and only travelled half as far. We should have changed a tyre." I drank a mouthful of water. "And I should be desperate to turn around, go back home to the city. Instead, I'm looking forward to getting to the old homestead."

Callie smiled at me. "Things are different now. Your parents are dead. All the ghosts are gone." It was a strange thing for her to say, because I had never told her about Yessmiss.

There was something familiar waiting for me at the homestead; something I had not seen for years.

"Yes," I said. "Yes, Miss." I used my sleeve to polish the dashboard.

"Yes, Miss," I said. The smell of furniture polish haunted me as a child; I smelt it when no one else did. I only use a cloth when I polish.

The smell of polish surely didn't get stronger as we drove further away from the city. I sniffed, though, sniffed again, and I could smell Yessmiss, my childhood ghost, as we drew closer and closer to the place of my birth.

Callie didn't speak. She drove, just crunch crunch of the road, crunch crunch of the barley sugar until her eyes watered. Without asking me, she pulled in at a pub. "Let's have a drink," she said.

She wasn't a country girl, she didn't realise what these places could be like. The social centre of a small town, where people behaved in established ways. Two women together were sluts looking for a root.

Pubs don't welcome strangers.

"Well, don't order a martini," I said. "Just a beer. Don't even specify which kind, just say beer."

Callie laughed. She grew up in the inner-city; she thinks she's tough. She leaned over and kissed me on the mouth. Her lips were sticky with barley sugar juice. I polished them with my tongue.

"Yes, Miss," she said. I had never explained my silly saying. Didn't need to with her. She just accepted it, embraced it. As she embraced me and my skittishness, my temper, my passions, my goals.

"This isn't the place to be out," I said.

"Der," she said, squeezing my thigh. "Really, you think you've cornered the market for narrow-minded. Mate, I've been abused in more places than you've. . ."

She couldn't think of a clever ending and I laughed.

"Than I've had trips around the world. Which is none."

"Won't be long," she said. We were travelling together in three months time, my last chance before the next career move tied me up for years. It would be our honeymoon, in advance.

But first I needed to watch the demolition of my childhood home.

#

There was a buzzy murmur as we entered the pub. Callie behaved beautifully, but I could see it annoyed her. I had suffered so much, I knew how cruel, how BLIND, these people could be.

There is always a young one in the pub, who gets a little sex every now and then from someone who isn't his wife, shoots more kangaroos because he can still steer and aim at the same time, he's a legend for his drinking. He's been brought up at the pub, there with his Dad from the age of five, rather than home with Mum, because all she does is whinge. If Dad gets a bit pissy he might belt you one, but he'll give you a dollar with it. He'll give you sips of beer, get you pissed till you chuck at twelve, then you'll beat the crap out of him on the day you turn eighteen and take his place at the bar.

I know this; this is the story of my father and my brother.

They never heard Yessmiss. I was the only one. It began with the smell of furniture polish. We didn't use it in the house; we used spit.

I could read by the time I was three. Dad read the paper aloud, he had to understand it, and I sat on his knee and followed his moving finger. Mum taught me all she knew, but I was desperate for more. I read everything that came into the house; Reader's Digest was my favourite, because it lasted a little while, and there were hundreds of them piled up in the dunny.

I never saw Yessmiss. I imagined her round and cuddly, taller than me. At night I dreamt she crawled into bed with me, and we held on tight while the usual noise went on. Just before I left home at sixteen I thought I saw her; I woke with my heart racing, darkest before the dawn as I often did. I glimpsed a bent figure, fumbling at my bedhead.

"Yessmiss," she said. "Yessmiss."

That was all.

#

The carpet in the pub was green, though it could once have been beige. A dishrag was close by and I dried a puddle of beer, rubbing it, rubbing.

"That'll do, thanks, love," the bartender said. "You'll make someone a good wife, elbow grease like that."

"Can I have some chips, please?" I said. "A coupla packs of salt 'n' vinegar and one barbecue."

He tossed them on the counter and I paid, munched away, because I didn't want to talk to Callie. They'd KNOW if we talked. They'd be able to tell.

"Just passin' through, are yous?" It was the young guy; he could have been my brother.

"Just seeing a bit of the countryside," Callie said.

"God's country, here," he said, and the bar murmured.

I glanced around; the door was propped open with the fire extinguisher; brilliant sunlight poured in, a broad strip. A black dog lay sleeping there, his ears flicking away the flies.

Apart from that the place was in darkness. There were no windows, only advertisements for beer, boxers, guns and Penthouse.

"God's country," I said, and raised my glass. Callie glared at me; she knows better than me when to put a stop to things.

The young guy took the stool next to me at the bar.

I polished the bar. "Yes, Miss," I said.

"Sorry, love?" said the young guy. He leaned close and I could see he wasn't so young. Mid 30s and nowhere to go.

"Buy you another?" he said.

"Nah, look, we've gotta head off," I said, and Callie and I downed our beers and stood up. I didn't know, until we were in the car, if they would let us go. I had forgotten how frightened I could be.

"Fuckin' lezzos," they said after us, which made us smile, then laugh, made it all worth it.

"So, what was all that about?" I said to Callie. "Why the tearing need to get our heads kicked in at a country pub?"

"I just needed a break."

"Oh, from me? Thanks a lot. I won't say anything if that's it."

We drove in silence while she thought of what to say.

"It's just that I don't always understand you. I thought if we broke it up a bit, you'd stop worrying."

"Well, it didn't work. It's worse."

"Well, I only tried." She was right; I had thought I was happy to be heading home, but she saw through my pretence. Yes, Miss, she did.

#

We were still five hours from the homestead, and I wanted energy for what came next, so we pulled into a motel, just three rooms, coffee and tea facilities and a huge fat candle to make things romantic.

The owner didn't flinch, putting us in the same room. We're such good friends, Callie and I, people don't assume we're lovers as well. And he had that tired look, that bored look, he didn't care anymore, he just wanted it to be over.

The bed sagged in the middle so we rolled together all night. We lay, lip to lip, breathing each other's air until we were dizzy. Then we kissed, lazy, salty kisses, and we touched warm fingers to warmer skin, we threw off the blankets and watched the candlelight against our lovely bodies. Nobody grunted and I didn't polish a thing. I do it in meetings; they mimic me, the others. Polish my glasses, or anything I can touch, the table, the coffee cup. They say if I stop polishing watch out!

I asked Mum once if she ever saw or heard Yessmiss, and I described her. Because she was clear in my mind. I knew what she looked like although I hadn't seen her.

Mum told me to stop eating cheese, it was giving me nightmares. In fact, she said, I needed to cut back all round if I was to be a lovely bride.

"Can girls marry girls?" I said, because I didn't ever want a husband, I wanted a wife.

A wife would laugh with me and be my friend.

A wife would smell nice.

Some things never change.

At school, I realised I was somebody; I was a Robey. My family had been in the district forever. We were the richies; we had servants, once. We were known for toughness, meanness, cruelty. If I ever asked anyone to do anything, they'd say, "Oh, yes, Mistress Robey, immediately."

Callie was very good to me. Very patient. She calmed me when I panicked. She talked to me a lot, the last five hours of the trip, made me laugh, let me be quiet and think. Yessmiss was waiting for me. I polished the windows to make sure we got there safely.

It was my first time home in fifteen years.

#

As we approached, I thought the front door was open, and I drew my breath, the fear of intruders too much.

"What is it?" Callie said. It was a favourite saying. "What is it?" I saw so many things she didn't see.

"There's someone in the house," I said, but when I looked again the door was closed. "It's okay," I said. "It's all right. I'm just remembering things. Let's go in."

I had a sticky key; hidden in a desk drawer these fifteen years. The door had not changed in that time; it was like I was returning from a week at school.

The front verandah hadn't changed.

"There's Dad's chair," I said. The imprint of his bum, decades of fat-arsed relaxing, had not left. He worked without cease, my Dad, until my brother was old enough, and then he sat down and hardly got up again.

"Once he stopped going to the pub he sat there for hours, drinking, shouting out at some ghost no one else could see."

Callie smiled at me, held my hand, tugged me close, kissed my cheek.

"I didn't realise you two had so much in common," she said.

"You'll have a ghost of your own one day, me, dead from neglect."

"Hardly."

The front door key was hot in my palm. I had had it ready to use for an hour now, my fingers pinching it, my wrist turning. I used it at last, and pushed open the door to my family home.

The smell of furniture polish would have made me gag if I were not so used to it. It made me remember how much I had forgotten about my childhood friend.

The house gleamed—shone—it was cleaner than I'd ever seen.

"Ooh, bit of dust there," Callie said, sarcastically. She didn't understand, so she joked.

"Yes, Miss," I heard.

It was Yessmiss. She was there.

Callie turned on the lights and we saw the stain in the thin, old carpet at the foot of the stairs where my mother had landed. I could imagine my father pushing her, because he'd done it before. But they were certain his heart attack had killed him three hours before she died; in that time she had fallen, dragged herself to the phone, and stayed alive long enough to reach hospital. She hated hospitals. They always asked questions about her injuries that were none of their business.

Callie explored the house. There was not much to look at; my siblings had cleaned the place out after the funeral. Piles of old Reader's Digests, a broken toy or two, furniture nobody would ever want, that's all they left. I sat upstairs, alone in my bedroom and waited for Yessmiss.

"Are you there, Yessmiss?"

"Yessmiss," my childhood ghost said. She was louder than I remembered, and a trick of light showed her to me. She was short, and broad, and familiar.

Callie and I ate toast cooked in the fire and drank red wine from plastic cups we found under the sink.

My old room had barely been touched. We slept that night in my single bed, where I had spent so many nights dreaming of this; a beautiful woman holding me perfectly. Callie always sleeps by the wall if there is one. Our king-sized bed at home has only one free side. She feels protected that way. She knows what's coming. Callie, I think, has stories of her own she doesn't tell.

Yessmiss woke me in the night. She was clearer in the moonlight. She polished the brass knobs of my old family bed, the one which had belonged to a spinster aunt when the house was first built and the family rich, a hundred years before.

That aunt was the main cause of our family's reputation.

Yessmiss polished and polished. "Yessmiss," she said, and "Yessmiss."

Then, and I could see this clearly now, I knew it wasn't a dream, she raised her hands to protect herself and fell to the floor.

I threw off the doona, crawled to the end of the bed. She was not there.

My heart beat quickly, too fast. Yessmiss had woken me out of deep dreaming, shocked me, and I wondered for a moment if she had appeared to my father as suddenly, and made his heart fail.

#

Callie loved the heat, sat out in it till her clothes sizzled. We ate sandwiches and toast, drank cuppa after cuppa sitting on the verandah.

Time passed. We were happy, unhassled, though we snapped a little at each other in the quiet of it all.

Then one morning we woke to banging downstairs. I pulled on some clothes and covered Callie with the doona. It was the wrecker, wanting to come look. My brother owned the house now, because girls didn't own houses. He hated it. Hated the age of it, so he was having it pulled down. A new house built, modern, with pastel colours and man-made materials.

The wrecker was a small, smelly man, neatly dressed in polyester shirt. Three or four days of sweat-stains under the arms looked like a map showing rainfall. His men were giants and worked in shorts, their backs bare, brown and marked with melanomas.

"Didn't think anyone was here," the wrecker said. He nodded at me.

Not his place to judge. He did a quick scout around the house, a first impression, he called it, while his assistants smoked, leaving the cigarette butts in a neat campfire pile. He caught Callie and me kissing in the kitchen; he rapped on the window.

"Hello, hello," he said. "Don't let us stop you."

"How do you do?" said Callie, turning to face him. Her voice is strong but gentle. The wrecker stared at her, then me.

"Well, well," he said. And that was it for niceties. "We'll be back next Thursdee."

#

Yessmiss appeared again and again. Callie couldn't see her at all; she watched me watching, and I caught her crying.

"She's there," I said. Yessmiss polished every night, I could see her. Had she always been there to be seen? As Callie and I tasted and touched, I heard her mutter, and there at the foot of the bed she was, she polished the ancient brass knobs then her hands flew to her head, her eyes locked with mine, she collapsed.

I stared at the space thinking it was real.

"What is it, love?" Callie said. I loved her for not adding, "this time."

"Murder," I said. "Murder."

I thought again about my father and how my mother would have found him and run down the stairs. Naked, I walked there; stood at the top and slid my feet over the smooth, slippery polished surface. I had my mother's habit of wearing socks to bed.

Yessmiss watched me. She held her head; seemed to be crying.

"Yes, Miss," I said.

She walked towards me.

I remembered how I dreamed of her, those lonely nights in my antique bed. She held her arms out to me but I didn't fear being pushed. I held my arms out and somehow she was whole, I hugged her and her flesh was sweet.

She passed her hands across my face and I was her, and my name was Agnes, and I worked for the spinster, the one who's photographic image was sour and unhappy.

I was her servant, my jobs were many, but mostly I had to polish. The Miss loved her things shiny and they were never shiny enough. My ears were boxed, my legs pricked with pins, she said, "Agnes, let's get a nice shine up. A nice shine," and I said, "Yes, Miss."

That's all. I didn't have other words. Some days she was even meaner and I was terrified for my life. And she slept in the bed with the brass knobs, and she liked them shiny first thing, shiny like the sun, and I get up in the dark to polish and polish, and one morning it's dark and she groans in her sleep, and the master of the house is within the bed, and he shouts at my presence when the moonlight strikes.

And she strikes me; and again.

And I polish and polish, as is my job. And I see a young girl, lonely like me, different like me, and she hears me.

She hears me.

She is the only one who does.

#

Agnes took her hands away and was gone. Callie called me and oh, how she loved me. She said, "Never mind, never mind," without needing to know what was wrong, and I realised she often spoke to me like that, warm short words like pats of comfort.

I promised myself to be good to her, understand her, allow her to be weak sometimes.

But I know I'll forget.

#

We packed all the things from my room. Dismantled the bed and strapped it to the roof. I whispered, "You shouldn't have killed them, Agnes. Not for me, anyway. But I wish you well. I hope you find another little girl."

Agnes paced back and forth across the room, her hands flapping.

I watched her until my eyes felt gritty with sand.

#

Callie and I sat in the air-conditioned car for three hours and watched men demolish the house. I thought of Agnes; I pictured her there, on her knees, polishing the floorboards. She was about to die again.

We went into town for lunch, came back, the house was almost gone. Such a simple, destructive thing. My brother wanted the land cleared.

He wanted every last bloody stick off it.

We drove away.

#

As we left, I felt something nestle around my neck, a cool, soft wreath I could lie my head against. I thought how much Agnes would love our house in the city; made of wood, full of it, and it's a warm, comfortable place. We allow things to pile up.

Callie says often, "For someone who loves to polish, you're a pig!" but she is like that too.

We both love a mess.

#

We were nearing home, after many hours, when Callie sniffed the air. Her brow creased, a rare sight.

"What is it?" I said.

"I smell furniture polish. Why would I suddenly smell furniture polish?"

I had never told her about the smell of Agnes. I had mentioned her, not her polish.

"I can smell it too," I said. I wondered how Agnes could possibly have known we were approaching her new home.

I would never bring her killer to justice, but I mourned her death and I felt the guilt for my ancestors.

That, it seemed, was enough. She forgave me, and my family, and once we were home I rubbed Callie's feet until she moaned.

ABOUT THE AUTHOR

Shirley Jackson award-winner Kaaron Warren is an ally (she/her) published her first short story in 1993 and has had fiction in print every year since.

She has published six multi-award winning novels: *Slights, Walking the Tree, Mistification, The Grief Hole, Tide of Stone and The Underhistory* and seven short story collections, her most recent being *Calvaria Fell,* with Cat Sparks, from Meerkat Press. Her stories have been shortlisted for the World Fantasy Award and the Stoker, and appeared in both Ellen Datlow's and Paula Guran's *Year's Best* anthologies.

Her writing podcast *Let the Cat In* showcases ideas, objects, and inspirations.
Her latest novel *The Underhistory,* from Viper Books, was described in the Guardian as 'a beautifully constructed, suspenseful gothic tale'.
Kaaron is an ally who lives on Ngambri and Nugunnawal land.

Bells At Winterdark

Kell Shaw

What if you could turn the world into a feel-good Winterdark movie? Imagine, no matter how bad things got, there would always be a happy ending with lovers embracing, enemies forgiving each other and villains admitting the errors of their ways.

That was why I accepted my dream job as a nephilim. A full time employee of the angels, my job was to assist my employers with making the world a better place for everyone. Oh, that's what I thought it would be like after my initial visitation and contract, where I was appointed a Reality Adjustment Technician, Tier One. I dreamed I'd put smiles on people's face, and see estranged parents embrace their children once more.

Instead, the sort of work I did was confusing, and didn't make a lot of sense. For example, the angels would ask me to leave a cup of coffee on a park bench or pretend my car had broken down in front of someone's driveway, delaying their departure by a few minutes. And while this might fit into the angels' big, incomprehensible plan for the universe, all I did was get scowls when a man spilled the coffee on his shirt, or irate yells and rude gestures for blocking a driveway.

Saddened, I asked the angels what my work really meant, by texting them in the App.

I received this message:

Good morning Mr. Arthyr 'Art' Marigold, Reality Adjustment Technician (Tier One) (he/him)

Thank-you for your enquiry. Please note:

1) We have a Plan.

2) The Plan focuses on the wellbeing of the world and civilization.

3) Recognize that all your work is to support the Plan.

4) We appreciate your time and service.

Thank you.

Angelic Employee Support Network

Second Hierarchy (They/Them)

I was sure what I was doing was useful, but it wasn't really wanted I wanted to be doing. I filled out all the survey forms and put in job requests, but got more adjustment assignments. Perhaps things would change when I'd built up enough positive reputation to be promoted to a higher tier and earn my wings. And I wanted my wings more than anything - to fly above the city and see everything spread before me like jewels had been a secret fantasy of mine from childhood.

And one day my dream mission came in. The support ticket read:

Good morning Mr. Arthyr 'Art' Marigold, Reality Adjustment Technician (Tier One) (he/him)

RE: New support ticket 215-Green-Pyramid

Assist [No Preferred Title] Ozariel [Last name classified] (Glorious Host Operative, Tier Three (he/him) (Status: suspended) with reinstatement into the Glorious Host.

Thank you.

Operative Assignment Delivery Network

Second Hierarchy (Xe/Xem)

Odd, to be assigned to assist another nephilim. I searched for Ozariel's public profile in the System. He dripped military awards, achievements and commendations. I found him at the Gateway Club sitting by alone, hands clenched around a bottle of plum wine. Ozariel was 'blended'—someone with human and ogre ancestry—and he resembled a prison lifer rather than war hero. Over two meters tall, with long matted hair and beard. Tattoos of skulls, arrows and spears covered his forearms.

"What do you want?" he growled when I appeared at his table. "You look like a salesman. Piss off."

As a Reality Adjustment Technician, I dressed to fade into the background and wore a crisp white shirt and tie. *Not* a salesman. At least I didn't look like someone who slept in a back alley.

I cleared my throat and showed him my System app. "I'm Art. A fellow employee. I'm here to help you."

Ozariel glared at me with bloodshot eyes. "Help me? *You?*"

"Yes." I clutched my phone.

Ozariel pointed a finger at my device. "That says you're Tier One. You don't even have your wings yet. I need an experienced agent, not some wet-nosed greenhorn."

"I wouldn't have been assigned to this ticket if our employers didn't think I could help."

"It's probably a glitch," Ozariel snapped. "Wouldn't be the first."

I had better things to do than spend time with a hostile, angry person. Like file a report on how this ticket was a complete waste of my time. "Well, I'm glad you know better than Upstairs. Good luck with whatever."

"Wait!" Ozariel stood, knocking the chair behind him onto the floor with a loud bang. Startled patrons paused their meals mid-bite or conversations to stare at us.

"I'm desperate. Let's talk." Oz twisted his huge hands together.

I folded my arms. "You'll be polite and decent?"

Ozariel nodded.

I pulled up a chair.

"Drink? Plum wine?" Oz grunted.

"A sugar-free lemonade would be nice."

Ozariel signalled a waiter.

"What is the problem, Ozariel?"

"Call me Oz. I'm suspended." He slammed down his empty glass and ordered another drink. "From the Glorious Host. Can't call down my wings or summon my holy sword. I messed up. I was fighting cambions. They're the demons' servants; scheming and plotting to break their infernal bosses out of the nether realm."

"I know what—"

"So who cares if there was an explosion or two? Those Reality Adjustment dweebs are there to tidy up after those of us in the Hosts."

"Well, it's delicate work and—"

"And what if some civilians nearly got hurt? They shouldn't have been there. Reality Adjustment should have. . ."

"Excuse me?"

"What? Did you say something?" Oz blinked at me with bloodshot eyes.

"I'm in Reality Adjustment." Was that what we did? Clean up after crazy agents like Oz? I glared at him over my lemonade.

"Whatever. To make amends, I have to clear this support ticket." He tapped his phone. "But it's impossible. It says I have to get two assets into a romantic relationship by Winterdark."

"Assets—you mean individuals?" I clutched the edge of the tale. The kind of assignment I'd always wanted, but never been given."

"Yes," Oz snorted. "Lily Lakeview and Josana Miller. Jo." Oz threw his phone on the table. "Bah! I eliminate threats. I don't mess around with mundanes' lives. How am I supposed to pull this off in the space of a week?"

"I can do this," I breathed. After all, I'd seen every Winterdark movie on the Festival Channel at least twice.

Oz glared at me, then sighed in resignation. "I might have misjudged you. Let's do a deal, Art. We'll be partners. You get me reinstated, and I'll put in a good word for you. You'll be jumping tiers and earning your wings in no time."

I shook his rough, calloused hand. "Agreed."

#

"The initial encounter is important," I told Oz. "They'll meet and instantly feel a connection to each other."

We planned Operation: First Contact for our clients. For a day, Oz tailed them in the field while I crunched through their information trails online.

Jo was an accountant for a large real-estate company; Lily was a middle manager at a bank. Both human, white collar, single, living in the same city, but unlikely to bump into each other without supernatural intervention. On social media photographs, Jo resembled a tortoise with her tiny, round-lensed spectacles and a fondness for patterned berets. Lilly had long, fashionably messy hair, and a fondness for elven fashions.

We contrived for them to be walking along the Peach Street Mall at the same time in the evening.

With six days left until Winterdark, the shops were full of fibreoptic bonfires. Children ran past with glowing toy swords, while others fired foam arrows at each other, pretending to be the legendary Heroes of the Hawkbow who had defeated the Dark Emperor on that fateful day two thousand years ago.

I sat on a park bench, listening to a busker playing steel drums on plastic tubs. Jo appeared first, shambling forward in a post-work fog, noise-cancelling earphones wrapped tight over her beret.

I checked my watch. 5:07pm. We needed Lily to come along at 5:08, where they would accidentally bump into each other and sparks would fly.

But Lily was nowhere in sight.

I phoned Oz. "Where is she?"

He picked up, out of breath. "She was about to leave the office but was delayed when someone asked her opinion about the upcoming election. She's leaving now. ETA ten minutes. I've got an idea. . . Stall turtle girl for me." He hung up.

To delay Jo, I would have to break cover.

"Wait!" I chased Jo as she walked past the busker. "I want to tell you about something important that could change your life forever."

"Not interested."

"I'm working on my start-up," I continued. Jo would have sympathy for this, she read tech magazines and liked contributing micropayments to support peoples' dream business plans. "It's for the ultimate dating app. You give me your details, you could be successful in love, win prizes. Whatever you want."

Behind her thick-lensed glasses, Jo's eyes gleamed like polished pebbles as she whipped out her phone. "What's the name of your app?"

In angel movies, they can pull off many convenient miracles, but my nephilim powers were far more limited. I couldn't make it rain rose petals, or magic up the perfect restaurant meal, or snap my fingers and conjure a house, but I could do little tricks with systems and machines. When I held out my phone, it displayed a landing page website:

Coming Soon! The ultimate in dating. Are you ready for the NEXT LEVEL? Sign up to learn more.

Jo scanned the QR code. "Tell me about your start-up."

"Well, it's a new concept in dating. It'll be a disruptive game-changer for the industry. Rather than awkward one-on-one partnerships and speed dates, we're going to pivot towards ubiquitous group meetings of compatible people, profiled with the latest in personality management tools, and—"

Ten minutes later, I was running out of the corporate buzzwords I knew. Oz arrived at the top of the mall, driving a sleek motorbike. A woman rode pillion behind him. When Oz pulled up, she removed her helmet, revealing glossy black curls. She handed the helmet back to Oz and walked away.

I had no idea how Oz had persuaded Lily to ride with him, but he'd done it.

Now for that first encounter.

I gave the signal to the trainee stuntwoman I'd hired earlier.

She pedaled forward and fell off her bicycle in front of Jo, who tripped over the spinning wheels and stumbled into Lily, dropping her phone in the process.

Both Jo and Lilly bent down to pick the phone up at the same time.

Their eyes met.

Jo picked up the phone, and handed it to Lilly.

"Thanks." Their gaze slid past each other.

Lilly strode on.

"Are you alright?" Jo asked the stuntwoman.

"Sure, all good." She righted the bicycle and pedaled onwards.

Jo opened her mouth, closed it, then shrugged and walked off in the opposite direction.

"That was it?" Oz appeared behind me. "They barely spoke to each other!"

"The first look is critical."

"You told me to expect an explosion!" He mimed a bomb going off. "Except that was a dud. Are you sure you know what you're doing?" Oz glared. "I've only got six days to get my wings and sword back."

I gritted my teeth. I would have to show him.

#

We went to my home that evening for important research.

"Is this a safe house?"

"It's my apartment."

"It's empty-looking."

White walls, designer furniture, everything clean. I couldn't see a problem. "I like minimalism. Now, let's watch this." I pulled out my collection of festival movies and played the best one: *Bells at Winterdark*.

Oz ordered pizza halfway through. "You know, it's not as good as *The Storming of Tower Nine* but it has its moments." He wiped his eyes when the main character commandeered a boat to the Haven Islands, to beg his love not to take up a two-year post as a lonely and isolated bell-ringer in a distant village. "Don't tell anyone in my unit that I'm enjoying this schmaltzy stuff."

I chewed on my slice of vegan cheese and tomato pizza, reflecting there had to be more to Oz. Then again, this movie was *that* good. After we finished, I reviewed the important scenes. "They meet, then they have another encounter where they get to know each other, and the third time, it's the magic at midnight; the moment then they kiss, or propose."

"What are you going to do next to the assets? Trap them in a basement?"

"I was thinking of an elevator."

#

After some rescheduling and reality adjustments, we arranged for Jo and Lily to be in the same elevator at Regal Department Store. I hacked the systems and waited as the doors sprung shut. For good measure, I cut their phone reception so they couldn't do anything except talk to each other and learn about each other's secret hopes and dreams.

Except, I hadn't realized that Lily was claustrophobic. That helpful tidbit had not been disclosed on her social media nor had it otherwise popped up during my research. If I'd known, I would have thought of another plan.

With Lily's loud, panicked yells echoing throughout the shopping centre, all Jo learned was that she didn't want to be near her. I restored systems, as the maintenance worker arrived and forced the doors open. Jo scurried out, while the maintenance woman spent half an hour talking to Lily about dogs to get her to calm down.

It was a disaster. Rather than uniting these women under a stressful moment, I'd pushed them apart.

Oz and I convened in the food court.

"Maybe you're right." I poked at my unappetizing avocado salad. "I don't know what I'm doing. Our set up and reality adjustments have been perfect, but it's not following through."

"You're trying to direct one of those crappy movies," Oz said through a mouthful of MegaBeef burger.

"They're not crappy movies. They're *happy* movies and remind people of what Winterdark is all about." I gestured at the commercial paraphernalia in the food court. Fiber-optic bonfires shone at the display at the centre. Cardboard cut-outs of the Heroes of the Hawkbow stood around them. People walked around in green, hooded cloaks, pretending to be the legendary adventurers. "That no matter how bad things got for our champions, they had faith in each other." I wiped my eyes, thinking of the last campfire the Heroes had shared together before the fateful Battle of Reladon.

"If I'd been there, I would have flown down and chopped the Emperor's head off with my holy sword." Oz watched a child run past, slashing the air with a plastic blade.

"Is flying fun?"

"The best. You can't imagine it." Oz looked up, a secret smile on his face.

I sighed. It would be a long time before I earned my wings.

Oz made embarrassing slurping noises as he drank his soda. "Maybe you're not playing to your strengths. What are you good at?"

"Systems, hacking, that sort of thing."

"So do that. Some computer stuff. Something that will work."

I pulled out my phone. The impromptu miracle I'd conjured earlier—the dating website—contained only one email address. Which was Jo's.

I *knew* she wanted romance. She and Lily would make a wonderful couple, if they gave each other a chance. But both were busy people who lived controlled lives. Maybe I should take a more hands-off approach.

"I've got it," I said. "Let's get this dating business started."

#

With the dating app, I set up a prize: a dinner on Winterdark Eve for Jo, Lily and a few other singles. I'd rented a restaurant for the occasion. Oz and I spent hours decorating it. He hung streamers from the ceiling, and I hooked up a recording of a bonfire that planed on wall flatscreens on loop.

Jo showed up in a terrible sweater with a campfire on it. Lily was fifteen minutes late, tossing her wild hair, wearing a hooded, green cloak.

I'd put in an open ticket on WorkGig for extras, and a small crowd had responded, including an ogre in a loud corduroy suit, a few humans in elven robes, an elf in a t-shirt who kept glaring at those humans, and of course, the stuntwoman from the bicycle trick, and the shopping centre maintenance worker who freelanced on the side.

Dressed in a cream, linen suit, I called Jo and Lily over and offered them complimentary sparkling wine.

Their eyes lit.

"It's you from the lift," Lily said.

"Yes," Jo said.

Ask how she is, I thought at Jo.

But Jo only grabbed her glass. A moment of awkward silence.

Lily took her drink and retreated to the far side of the restaurant.

I had one evening to get these people to fall in love. They needed to learn more about each other until the magic of romance drew them together. I spent hours hosting party games where they learned about each other's hopes and dreams, and where possible, I arranged for Jo and Lily to be on the same team. During a break, I went back into the kitchen for a quick sugar-free lemonade. Oz was standing there, arms folded.

"You know, I don't think Jo and Lily have much in common," I said. "Lily likes dogs, Jo prefers cats. Lily's into going out for movies, while Jo would rather invest in a complete home theatre system. It's not even opposites attract—it's more like they have nothing to say to each other."

"I need to get my holy sword back." Oz interrupted my musing.

"This isn't about you, or your sword." My voice was a trifle too sharp. "This is about making two lonely people *connect* in ways they normally wouldn't. Aren't you here because you're more interested in chopping up cambions than saving civilians?" I waved a hand at the crowd who were drunkenly playing the egg-and-spoon race up and down the restaurant. "Are you even paying attention?"

Oz pointed to an orc in dark sunglasses leaning against the far wall. "He's not on the guest list."

The intruder saw us watching him. Smiled. And pulled out a glowing, blinking device in his hands. Was that—a *bomb detonator?*

"It's Riven, a two-bit terrorist. If I had my holy sword right now, I could take care of him."

"Well, you don't," I said. "I'm going to talk him out of it—"

"Talk?" Oz snapped. "You can't talk to a cambion—"

"Not listening." I left the kitchen and edged around the corner of the restaurant to confront Riven. Cambions could appear in a demonic form with scaled skin and horns, but Riven appeared like your average orcish biker thug with bronze-capped tusks and piercings through his porcine ears.

"Hello. What are you doing?"

"Ruining your nephilim op." Riven lowered his sunglasses, revealing red-glowing eyes. "I don't know what you're planning, but Ozariel has killed enough of my dark legion buds to make me want to blow this place sky high."

"Stop that." I performed a system miracle to shut down the detonator. "This is a *festival op*. We're trying to get these mundanes to fall in love with each other." I pointed at Jo, who was showing off her new phone to the stuntwoman, and Lily, who was asking the maintenance worker about her dogs. Both at opposite ends of the restaurant from each other. "Oh no, they're not talking to each other. Again."

"Festival op?" Riven leaned forward. "Like some crappy Winterdark movie?"

"Yes."

The cambion indicated Oz, who had followed me. "You expect me to believe that?"

"He got demoted. Lost his wings—"

"Shut up, Art—" Oz growled.

"And his holy sword—"

"Will you shut up?"

The cambion laughed. "You, Ozariel the Indomitable, on *festival duty?*"

Oz snapped and stretched out his hands. If he could have called his sword, it would have appeared.

But it didn't.

"This is the best Winterdark present ever," Riven crowed. "And you know what, salesneph? Your op is dead in the water. I can't smell any desire for each other from those mortals." Sniggering, he put away the bomb detonator and pulled out his phone, chatting into it as he left the restaurant. "Hey Ral? You won't believe this. Ozariel's been demoted. He's such a loser!"

Oz's muscles bulged under his tuxedo.

I placed a restraining hand on his shoulder.

The cambion laughed, made a rude gesture, and left.

I swallowed. "Time to play charades. It's less than an hour until midnight!"

Yes, an hour to the miracle moment. It *would* happen! I'd make sure of it! I pushed the group into round of truth or dare where they revealed even more of their secret hopes and dreams to each other, and then, at 11:44pm, I played slow, romantic dance music and sat in a corner, closing my eyes and sipping my sugar free lemonade. Time to let things happen

Outside, the city bells struck midnight. Around the land, people were kissed, swore vows or watched fireworks.

I opened my eyes.

Everything was wrong.

Jo slowly danced with the stuntwoman, and Lilly sat in the corner, showing the maintenance worker pictures of dogs on her phone.

They pair hadn't even looked at each other all night.

I told everyone the night was over and thanked them for coming. Couples and throuples left to get chocolate. I gritted my teeth as Jo and Lilly departed—with other people.

At 12:15, only Oz and I were left alone in the restaurant. "Thanks, Art. For nothing." He didn't even meet my eyes as he collected his motorcycle jacket from the coat hook and slipped it on over his tuxedo. "This op was a bust. I should never have listened to you."

#

I spend a few hours cleaning the restaurant, putting chairs on tables and vacuuming. When I got home, I couldn't sleep. I tried to watch 'Bells at Winterdark' with a bottle of sugar-free lemonade, but the movie was as emotionally satisfying as wet cardboard. I was numb, burnt-out and all I could do was brood on how cruel the world was, despite my best intentions.

I'd never enjoy a romantic movie again.

At 3:30am, there was a tap on my window.

I slid it open.

Oz was outside. Fifty meters above street level, suspended by glowing silver wings.

"You got your powers back?"

"You bet. I reread my support ticket. It said that the two assets had to be in a romantic relationship at the end of the period. I assumed that meant with each other."

"You *assumed*—" I took a deep breath and exhaled. I was so drained that I couldn't even feel angry at Oz's inability to read a simple support ticket.

"Well, I'm glad you're sorted. Good night, I mean, good morning." I moved to close the window.

But Oz stretched out and took my hand in his rough, firm grip. "Come. I'll show you what it's like to fly."

ABOUT THE AUTHOR

Kell Shaw is an author and avid tabletop roleplaying gamer, whose lifelong passion for fantasy—especially Shadowrun, the Lord of the Rings, and the World of Darkness—inspired him to create the Vestiges of Magic urban fantasy universe. Kell's fascination lies with the modern world colliding with magic, and his stories explore the lives of individuals caught between these realms.

Identifying as queer, Kell is committed to writing diverse characters who embark on thrilling adventures, and who aren't defined by their love lives. He released the first book of the Revenant Records saga in 2022, following an undead teenage detective who wants to grow up despite being forever seventeen.

Based in Sydney, Australia with his partner and beloved feline companion, Kell's diverse career has included roles as a technical writer, risk analyst, and project manager.

Sign up for Kell's newsletter at https://kellshaw.com/newsletter to receive free short stories and stay up-to-date with his latest projects.

What A Ghoul Wants

Rowan Dale

Poppy's heart had led her many places most people wouldn't go with a gun, a knife, and a crate full of explosives. She looked up at the dilapidated prison, shading her eyes with her forearm. It was massive and old in a way few things on the frontier were. Even a Big would call this place huge. To a halfling like Poppy the scale was staggering. Late afternoon sun glinted off the few panes of glass still stuck in the arched windows, and the stone façade was baked white from years of desert sun. The roof bowed in the middle like a crooked smile, and Poppy wondered how many ghosts you could fit inside forty-one thousand square meters.

Beside her, Edwood whistled. "You sure know how to pick 'em, Poppy. I don't think most folks would go in for exorcising a place just for a date."

Poppy's cheeks burned. "Forsythia isn't just any woman."

Edwood rolled his eyes. "You met her a week ago. You've spoken all of a dozen words to her, total."

Trust a gnome like Ed not to understand true love when it came knocking. Or came barrelling into you like a dust storm. Poppy was used to dodging Bigs, given that the frontier was made up of way more of them than of Smallfolk like herself. But Forsythia moved like a storm, overcoming her in a flurry of skirts, knocking her into the dirt. When she resurfaced from all those layers of frills, she'd found herself eye-to-eye with the finest woman in all the West. Eyes like polished amber, hair the colour of caramel, and a mouth ripe as a fresh cherry. The sight of her would have taken Poppy's breath away if she wasn't already gasping from suffocating under three layers of cotton and taffeta.

"You'd be surprised how little folks need to say to one another before they get to tumbling into the nearest bed, or alley." Roscoe swaggered up beside her, arms full of a jumble of trinkets and candles. Poppy bit the inside of her cheek to keep from calling him an unromantic idiot. This was the one time she needed to keep from arguing with him. She didn't know anyone else who was qualified to lead an exorcism, and she meant to exorcise this whole prison for Forsythia.

Roscoe was like most halfling men: happy to sweet talk a gal, or a guy, into a roll in the hayloft, but always slipping out before dawn. He was blessed with one of those sweet faces that was as likely to steal the heart of a Big as any halfling or gnome maiden, with his rosy cheeks and messy honey-blonde hair. There was nothing about him that hinted at his predilection for witching, and he never took any of his lovers near his wagon full of charms and potions. They'd be proper spooked by the number of animal skulls he owned.

Then there was Ed, the least gnomish gnome she'd ever met. She doubted he even owned one of the coloured pointed caps all his kin wore. He was all sharp angles, his jaw stubbled, his skin a warm brown. He looked more like a Big than a gnome, if you ignored the pointed ears and the fact that he was even shorter than her. As for romance, he had zero interest in it. Hells, she'd never even seen him smile anyone's way, let alone offer them a piece of his frozen-over heart.

She wished she had anyone else she could ask to help her with this, but given she hung out with nothing but fellow criminals her pickings were slim.

"Shall we, gentlemen?" Poppy flung an arm out, trying to act like she wasn't trembling in her boots at the thought of entering the place.

"We'll have those ghosts out before they know what hit em," Roscoe beamed at her, showing off his dimples. "You'll be out of here before the moon's even full up, and into your gal's arms."

Poppy rolled her eyes. "We'll see about that."

She strode forward with all the false bravado of someone who didn't want you seeing their knees were shaking. Ed scampered after her, fingertips poised at the holster of his pistol just in case something attacked them. Roscoe, being Roscoe, followed them with an easy gait, like he was rocking up to a nice dinner rather than a haunted prison.

The grounds were all grey stone and displaced gravel. There wasn't a single tree or bush, not a bit of sun-dried grass. The paint on the front door was peeled and curling, and gave the impression of something large and clawed using it as a scratching post. A heavy chain was wrapped around the handles, a rusty padlock hanging from it like the jewel on a giantess's necklace. Poppy fished a couple pins from her tangle of auburn hair and stood on her tiptoes, fitting the two ends into the lock. Picking the lock steadied her nerves a touch. It was familiar, easy. After a few pokes and turns the lock clicked and she pulled it free, unlooping the chains. The door was heavy, and it took her and Ed a whole lot of huffing and pressing with their shoulders to force it open. The screech of the hinges echoed in the cavernous insides of the building, setting Poppy on edge. She didn't like the thought of ghosts, or whatever else might be lurking in these dusty halls. Poppy preferred things that could bleed to anything that a bullet could pass through. She patted the silver knife tucked into her belt, hoping that the trader she'd bought it from was right and it could take down a ghoul.

They stepped into a long hall lined with cells, their doors half-open, lines of rust staining the wood like trails of blood. Dust motes danced in the air and the smell of damp and mould permeated the place like a rotten perfume.

"Well ain't this just cosy," Ed grumbled, taking in the heavy iron locks hanging off the doors. "What kind of prison is this anyway?"

"The Bigs built it during their war," Poppy said, wincing at the way the heels of her boots clicked with every step. "According to Forsythia it ended up housing the folks who learned that they liked soldiering, or rather the killing part, a little too much."

Edwood sucked a tooth. "Shit, Poppy. I've never faced a murderer I couldn't plug full of holes. You sure about all this?" He was stoic as always, but there was a clear undertone of unease in his words.

A loud clatter made them both jump out of their skin. They turned as one, Poppy wrenching her knife from her belt, Ed drawing his gun.

"Hey, I can't exorcise anybody if I'm dead," Roscoe said with a laugh, hands held up in mock-surrender. He'd dropped all his kit on the ground and sat sorting through the jumble of strings and herbs and gods knew what else. "You two sure are twitchy. The sun hasn't even set yet!"

Ed groaned and shoved his gun back in its holster. Poppy shot Roscoe an annoyed look. Normal folks didn't smile when they were in a place that was so haunted it lay abandoned for thirty years. But he was enjoying himself.

"You get your stuff sorted," she snapped. "Me and Ed will take a look around." She'd feel more comfortable when she had the lay of the place.

"Sure," Roscoe cocked his head to the side, fixing her with his most annoying smirk. "Keep an eye out for any signs of haunting. You know, writing on the walls, blood smears, stuff like that. If you need me just scream really loud."

Poppy huffed and turned on her heel. She realised she was still holding her knife and thought about sheathing it. But she felt better with it clutched in her fist, the hilt rough and reassuring against her palm.

She took the lead, marching down the length of the hallway, peeking behind the half-open doors. Cots leaned on broken legs, covered in rotting blankets, and shadows swarmed the corners of every room, deepening as the sun drooped towards the horizon. There was plenty of graffiti scratched into the cold stone walls: sometimes just marks for the days spent captive, other times it was names and old curses like the ones her pa used. It was soldier talk, the kind of coarse stuff that fit in on campaign but not at home. Not that it had ever stopped her pa. He'd been rougher than a wildcat, and just as prone to getting into scraps. She'd pulled enough bits of glass out of his palms, scrubbed enough cuts with alcohol to clean them out after he got into brawls down at the saloon. She'd been his little nurse, stitching him up with her ma's old sewing kit and telling him off like she was a disapproving mother rather than a frightened daughter. Her throat tightened at the thought of her old man, ten years buried under the old chestnut tree back home.

"This place is like a torture chamber in some half-copper horror story," Edwood ran a finger over a rusted washbasin. A set of surgical tools lay beside it, dissolving into the scrap of linen they'd been set upon, staining it russet. This room must have been the surgery. It was bigger than the cells, though no less bleak. An operating bench took up the middle of the room, the wood darker in parts. The floor was covered in clumped sawdust. "What does your gal want with this place anyway?"

Poppy picked up an old glove, noting the gore soaked into the fingers of it, and tossed it into the corner. "She wants to fix it up, turn it into a hospital."

Forsythia had told her all about her grand plans for a hospital fit to service the whole region. Folks could come from all the surrounding towns and homesteads to get patched up. She was even thinking of turning part of it into a ward just for the women, where they could birth babies and get a break from their menfolk. She'd include a parlour filled with books and nice chairs, where they could put their feet up and recover with a cup of tea and a good chat.

Poppy's heart had swelled with every word, and when Forsythia mentioned the dilemma with the hauntings Poppy had blurted that she knew an exorcist, offering to clear the place out for her. Never mind that Roscoe was more witch than exorcist, and about as godly as an imp. The way Forsythia's features softened at her offer had made her heart run wild as a prairie horse, and that made this whole scheme well worth it.

"She sounds like a real bleedin' heart," Ed said, turning his attention to a set of bottles in a caddy by the window. He picked one of them up, holding it up to the fading light, watching bits of flotsam bob within the liquid. "I'm surprised you're into that sort of thing."

Poppy heard the note of disapproval in his voice. She frowned. She didn't need Ed's approval. He was her friend, but sometimes he acted like he was her older brother, trying to give her advice that sounded a lot like scolding.

"You noticed anything strange yet?" She asked, eager to change the subject. "I haven't felt any ghosts." The hairs on the back of her neck weren't raised, and she had no goosebumps, which she took as a good sign. But then, it was light out. Once the sun was gone, she was sure she'd be jumping at every breeze through the broken windows, every scrabble of vermin across the floorboards. She started from the operating room and headed for a set of metal stairs spiralling up to the second floor. They were so thick with rust that a Big's foot would fall clean through them, but she was a halfling, and a fleet footed one at that, so she had no trouble scampering up. The patter of Ed's boots behind her was reassuring.

She emerged in another hall, this one even more decayed than the ground floor. Here the paint fell in clumps, exposing the bare stone of the walls. The floorboards were thick with dust and grime and creaked underfoot. The shadows were thicker too, and the window beside the stairs was blocked out by a heap of old bedframes and broken bits of furniture.

They started down the hall, their boots crunching on broken glass. The sun was so low that Poppy's vision was starting to get tricky. The door down there didn't move a fraction just then, did it? She squinted, trying to get a proper look.

"Poppy?" Ed's voice was low, a whisper. The hairs on the back of her neck stood on end at the sound. She turned her head and saw where he was looking.

It emerged from within the debris, one long arm creeping out, fingers dragging at the floorboards. A thick torso followed, and a misshapen head of featureless shadow.

It moved with surprising speed for something without legs, hauling itself towards them with purpose.

Nope, nope! Without thinking, Poppy grabbed Ed by the collar and yanked him into the nearest cell, slamming the door shut. Her heel caught on something hard, sending her sprawling to the ground. She took Ed down with her.

"What are you doing?" Ed hissed, scrambling to his feet. His eyes darted to the door, chest rising and falling in panicked breaths. She followed his gaze, watching as the door rattled but held. Whatever that ghoul out there was, it was inept at passing through doors. Not a ghost then, but something else.

Several bangs sounded, each one making Poppy flinch as the creature beat its shadowy fists against the wood. It gave up and moments later they heard the unsettling shuffle and drag of it hauling itself further down the hallway.

"What was that thing?" Ed's voice came out choked from a corner of the room, his gun drawn in shaking hands.

She got to her feet and dusted herself off, then retrieved her knife, which had been catapulted across the room when she fell. As she tucked it back in her belt, something lying on the floor of the otherwise bare cell caught her eye. It was a book, pages open, a little strip of cloth pressed in the centre of the spread to keep the reader's place. She lifted it, and the spine gave a little under the weight of the damp-bloated pages. The words were blurry, but still readable. She closed the book, examining the cover. The embossed lettering on the front was furry with mould. *The Gunslinger's Secret Bride.* She felt a pinch of recognition in her chest. Poppy remembered reading this book back when she was a girl, hiding up in the chestnut tree. She'd filched it from Mrs. Bakewell down the street. That old biddy had a whole host of romance novels tucked in her well-appointed parlour. Poppy spent many afternoons with her nose pressed to the window, reading all the titles on the coloured spines, before she worked up the courage to slip inside and stuff one of them down the front of her shirt.

She put the book down, her throat a little tight. It was books like this that had filled her head with ideas of grand romances. Looking at one of them now, she felt exposed, and childish. It was romantic ideas that got you killed by ghouls in abandoned prisons.

"You done reading?" Edwood groused. "I'd like to get out of here before that thing figures out how to open a door."

Poppy nodded and grabbed the door handle, giving it a tug. It didn't budge. She swore under her breath and gave it a proper yank. Not so much as a rattle. "It's locked."

"Then unlock it," Edwood said, arching a brow.

"I can't," Poppy said, cold dread washing over her at the realisation. "It's a prison cell, Ed. It only unlocks from the outside."

The colour drained from Edwood's face.

"I think this is the part where we start screaming really loud," Poppy said. "And hope that Roscoe knows a spell for undoing locks."

"What if that ghoul comes creeping back?" Edwood's voice was raw with fear. He was handling all this worse than Poppy was, and gods-knew she was ready to kick out a window and shimmy down a wall like this was a proper prison break. But, given how high up the single window in the room was, she doubted either of them could reach it, even if she stood on his shoulders.

"I think Roscoe can handle a ghoul," Poppy tried to sound like she believed her own words. "He has his witching, doesn't he? He can probably banish it straight to the hells with a flick of his wrist."

"He's a witch, not a priest," Ed snapped. "And that thing might not be a ghoul, or a ghost, or anything like that. What if it's a demon? He can't very well fight a demon on his lonesome, can he? You know how bad a shot he is."

Poppy rubbed her arm, over the scar from one of Roscoe's bullets that had ricocheted. She was lucky it hadn't struck her in the chest that night. "At least in here there's nothing living for him to hit by accident."

Ed's look was all acid. "You sure you can't get us out of here?"

"I'm a lockpick," Poppy snapped back, waving an arm at the iron-wrought door. "And this thing is annoyingly free of locks."

She examined the door, searching for any loose bits that could be jimmied with a knife or taken apart with a bit of force. It looked sturdy considering the surroundings. The only thing that stood out was a tiny hatch at the bottom of the door, for guards to shove food through. It was far too small for a Big to fit through, but a halfling and a gnome should be able to squeeze through. Just. She knelt down and studied the screws holding the hatch together.

"Do you hear that?" Ed asked, keeping his gun close to his chest like a kid might do with a comforting teddy.

Poppy paused, hands resting on the hatch. A distant scream echoed through the building. Goosebumps prickled up her arms and she shuddered. It didn't sound like a person. More like a trapped animal. Gods, would it be too much to ask for it to *actually* be an animal and not another ghoul?

She pulled out her knife and worked the tip under one of the screw heads. The metal was so rusted that it had a bit of give. She wiggled the screw free, and it landed on the ground with a satisfying ping. As she worked on the remaining screws, she became aware of a breathy sound beyond the door, like someone was pressed against it, panting. She flicked a glance at Edwood. He was watching the door, mouth set in a hard line. His pointed ears twitched with every phantom breath. She hoped to the hells that he was still a good shot when he was panicked like this. She'd seen him handle gun fights in the street and scuffles on the tops of moving trains without losing his cool. But right now, his cool had packed up and left town and it didn't look like it was coming back any time soon.

Plink after plink sounded, echoing, as the screws came loose under her knife. She heard the creature's every breath through the wood. How could it breathe? Wasn't it supposed to be dead? Where in the hells was Roscoe when they needed him? He knew a damned sight more about hauntings than she did.

She nodded to Ed, slipping her knife away, one hand pressed against the hatch to keep it in place. He bobbed down beside her, stuffing his gun back into its holster. She lowered the hatch, laying it to the side. They both looked at the small hole in the door, and Poppy wished she hadn't had so many cakes when she took tea with Forsythia.

"Ladies first," Edwood said.

She scowled at him and got down on her hands and knees. The floor was gritty, sharp bits of broken glass and crumbled plaster prodding her through her trousers. She took a deep breath, sending out a silent prayer to any gods that might still be on her side. Poppy didn't want to die stuck halfway through a door, devoured by ghouls.

She lowered herself onto her belly and stretched an arm through the hole. Something warm grabbed her forearm and she screamed, trying to back out. Her head smacked against the wood of the door, and she saw stars.

"Calm down, it's just me!"

Poppy swore, rubbing the back of her head and feeling a lump forming. "Curse you, Roscoe! You damn near stopped my heart!"

"I thought you needed a hand," he chuckled, his voice muffled.

"Instead of scaring folks half to death, how about opening the door?" Edwood offered; his tone clipped. But for all his annoyance, there was relief in the drop of his shoulders.

There was a rattle and thunk as the latch came undone and the door groaned open. Poppy and Edwood darted out of the cell so fast they collided with one another.

Roscoe was watching them, arms crossed, a smug grin plastered on his face. "How'd you two manage that then? Locking yourselves in a cell?"

"She dragged me in there," Edwood said.

Poppy rolled her eyes. Like he wouldn't have done the exact same thing. "There was a ghoul," she explained. "Didn't you see it when you came up?" She cast a glance down either side of the hallway expecting to see it dragging itself across the floor towards them. But besides the creep of shadows swarming around the dying flickers of sunlight through the windows there was no sign of anything, living or undead.

"Oh, you mean that one?" Roscoe cocked his head to the side and pointed to the ceiling. Poppy looked up and spotted the creeping ghoul clinging to a crack in the paint, tendrils of darkness dripping from its misshapen body like black wax. She damn near ran right back into the cell, but Roscoe put a hand on her shoulder, his touch reassuring.

"It won't hurt you," he said, watching as the ghoul observed them with its featureless head leaning to one side. "It's probably more scared of you than you are of it."

She doubted that. It could probably smell the witchiness coming off Roscoe and decided trying to eat them wasn't worth the risk of exorcism.

"Can we just get to the part where we banish all the ghouls and ghosts?" Edwood asked. He'd crept close to the two of them, pressing himself against Roscoe's side. Roscoe looped a comforting arm around Ed's waist, on instinct.

"Of course," Roscoe said, leading them both back to the stairs. Poppy felt a prickle on her neck the whole way, a keen awareness of the ghoul hanging just out of her periphery. "I've got everything set up. Though I reckon we have a chat with the residents before we start banishing. Seems the decent thing to do, don't it?"

Poppy shook her head. Trust Roscoe to treat the undead like living people. They returned to the main entrance on the ground floor. Roscoe had drawn a circle out of dirt, which she was sure came from someone's grave if the heebie-jeebies she got at the sight of it was any indication. Candles burned along the outside of the circle and the air was heavy with the scent of rosemary and lavender. Roscoe led them both into the circle and sat them down, so they were all facing one another. He produced several lengths of red string from his trouser pocket and made them hold their hands out, then he wrapped the strings around their hands, looping them onto each finger. She tried not to think about the metallic stench that rose from those strings or the way the old blood used in their making would rub off on her skin.

"That ought to protect the both of you," Roscoe said, trying off the strings and cutting the ends with his knife.

She looked to Edwood. He looked uneasy but didn't say anything. For all that he didn't like - or understand - magic, he trusted Roscoe. Those two were ride or die in a way Poppy couldn't quite wrap her head around. She dreamt of the day she found someone she could trust like Roscoe and Ed trusted each other. But she was sure that she'd only find that kind of bond with the love of her life. Perhaps, she thought, Forsythia would be that person for her.

Roscoe snapped his fingers, and the candle wicks burst into flame, casting the hallway in warm light. Magic churned up the air like a swarm of mosquitos. Her skin tingled like she was being pricked with a thousand tiny needles. Roscoe held his hands out, palms upturned, and they all linked hands.

Roscoe spoke, his words strange to her ears. They felt ancient, and wrong, like something that should have been left in the ruins of some desecrated city in the Elder Lands. Every hair on her body stood on end, and she didn't know if it was from Roscoe's words or the ghouls creeping just beyond the light of the circle. She heard scrabbling along the floor, the drag of bodies across wood. Beyond the light of the candles shapes shifted in the darkness. There had to be at least a dozen of them crawling out from the cells, from the cracks in the walls and the ceiling. They crowded around the circle, the light flickering as they reached for the candles. Their spindly shadow hands came apart under the candle flames and they hissed, shifting back, their misshapen heads cocked at strange angles. She was aware of them watching the three of them, soft whispers passing between them. They must be discussing which of them to eat first.

"What do you want to ask them?" Roscoe's voice was too loud, and Poppy leapt out of her skin. All at once, the ghouls fell silent.

He was looking at her, his blue eyes aglow with magic. She swallowed a lump in her throat, trying to think of something to ask. Would it be rude to ask them if they could just leave? Maybe a little threat of exorcism would make them high tail it out onto the plains.

She let out a breath, looking out over the congregation of ghouls. "Ask them what they want."

Roscoe's smile was softer than usual, almost genuine. "You heard her. What do you want?"

One shadow rose up, head peeking above the others. Its voice was thin and shrill, like the whistle of wind through broken glass. "You come to steal from us."

Edwood scoffed. "As if there's anything in this rotten dump worth looting."

Poppy shot him a warning look.

"We mean you no harm," she said, her voice shaking. "We came here to talk."

"Liar," another voice hissed. "Halflings came with foul magic. Came to hurt us."

Poppy swore inwardly.

"It's true," Roscoe said, his voice even. "We were sent here to clear this place out. But I'd rather you left on your own."

There was a collective hiss that made Poppy's head hurt.

"Are you the spirits of the prisoners who were kept here?" she asked.

"No," one of them said, its voice an octave higher than the first, but no less unsettling. "We came after, to feed on the pain, the screams that lingered. It has been long since we devoured the last of it."

Poppy shuddered, not allowing herself to think too much about what feeding on pain entailed. "If you have already done. . . that, then. . . something else must be keeping you here," she reasoned. "What is it?"

They turned their heads this way and that, as if exchanging glances. The tallest of them trembled where he stood. "We came to feed. We stay because this is where we shared the tale."

There was a chorus of hisses of agreement.

"The tale is ours. You will not take it from us."

"What are they talking about?" Edwood asked, frowning at the sea of shifting black. "There's nothing here. Nothing but broken furniture and rotting medicine."

And a book.

"You're talking about *The Gunslinger's Secret Bride*."

A dozen oblong heads turned in her direction.

"You're the ones who have been reading the book upstairs, aren't you?" She sat up a little straighter, looking at their leader. She swore it nodded at her words. "What's so important about it?"

"We cannot leave without knowing," the lead ghoul snarled. "If Jebediah Cottonwood saves Angelica Rue from the bandit leader."

Poppy blinked, their words sinking in, conjuring up memories. It had been years since she'd read *The Gunslinger's Secret Bride*. But now she remembered it like she was in the chestnut tree just yesterday, the book open against her knees. She'd been furious when she'd realised the first book ended in a cliffhanger. Mrs. Bakewell had the other three books in the series on her shelf, but breaking in a second time proved difficult. The old biddy had locked her windows against the strong winter wind off the plains, and Poppy hadn't been patient enough to wait for summer, when the windows would be open and easy to slip through. She'd taken her father's hunting knife and used it to pry the lock on the window open. That was where it all began: with a teenaged girl desperate to find out if a gunslinger and a runaway holy sister lived happily ever after. She'd spent the rest of her life chasing stories and picking locks. She was a runaway herself, a girl who believed that out there, somewhere, was her own happily ever after.

It was so quiet in the dark prison that she could hear the beat of her own heart. "You want to know how it ends?"

"Yes," the ghouls hissed. "We will not leave this realm until we know."

Roscoe and Edwood exchanged disbelieving looks. They'd both needled her about her love of romance novels for years.

"I know how they end," she said. "I could tell you."

The ghouls hissed, bunching together in a clot of blackness.

"Do not spoil it for us!" their leader hissed. "We want to share the tale. All of us."

Of all the things she'd thought they'd find here; a pack of well-read ghouls was not it. But at least this was something she understood, something she could do something about. No exorcisms necessary.

"I have the books," she said. "I haven't touched them in years, but I never had the heart to part with them. I could loan them to you if you promise to leave this place after you've read them."

The ghouls whispered between themselves, the sound like a fistful of nails hitting glass. Poppy grit her teeth. Roscoe gave her hand a reassuring squeeze, then bumped his shoulder against Edwood's, urging him to do the same. The three of them sat like that, their fingers intertwined, enchanted string rubbing against skin, as they waited for the ghouls to make their decision.

"We have considered your proposition," the head ghoul said, rising up even higher, its elongated head grazing the ceiling. It stretched its arms out, long tendrils of shadow snaking from its fingertips. "And we agree to your terms. Bring us the books, halfling, and leave us to read them in peace."

Poppy nodded to Roscoe. "Can I safely leave the circle?"

"They seem pretty docile," Roscoe said. "But keep the cords on. The last thing we need right now is a possession. I'm terrible at those."

Poppy slipped her hands free from the two of them and got to her feet shakily. The ghouls watched her step out of the circle, dodging the naked flames. They loomed over her and cold dread coiled around her guts. She clenched her fists, feeling the tug of the strings against the lines of her finger joints. The ghouls moved back, letting her pass through the hall, down to the door. She was aware of every step across the scuffed floorboards, of the distance opening between her and her friends. She stepped out into the night, letting the light of the moon guide her through the prison gates and out to the spindly trees where they'd tied their horses and wagon. It was dark under the canvas of the wagon, but she had no trouble finding the loose board or the books hidden underneath. She knew them by touch alone: the creases on the spines, the bold lettering embossed on the covers, the smell of old paper and the peppermint tea she'd spilled on the pages of book three. Poppy pressed the books to her chest, grounded by the weight of them against her breastbone. She walked back to the prison, slipping through the door and sighing a breath of relief when she spied Roscoe and Edwood still seated in the magic circle. The ghouls spied the books and came barrelling towards her in one heaving mass.

Poppy held the books tight, frowning. "Remember our bargain. Once you've read them, you'll leave this place."

A spindly arm reached out from the tangle, long fingers unfurling. "Give us the book, halfling girl. Leave this place for one turning of the moon. When you return, we will be gone."

She hesitated. Would the books survive a month in this damp place? She thought of the copy of book one upstairs, woolly with mould. She'd had these books since she left home. Could she part with them now, for the sake of some ghouls?

Not for the ghouls, for Forsythia. For all that she would do to this place, the people she would help. Poppy wanted to be there to see her dream come true.

She held the books out and three more arms shot out, multiple sets of dark fingers grasping the books.

"We thank you, halfling girl," the ghouls said in unison, their voices overlapping in an eerie chorus. They shifted away from her, dragging their clumped bodies up the spiral stairs, vanishing into the impenetrable darkness.

"Oh thank the ancestors that's over," Edwood huffed, hopping to his feet. Roscoe led him out of the circle and with another snap of his fingers the lights guttered out, trailing wisps of smoke. The moonlight cutting through the door led them to freedom and they hurried back to their wagon.

"So, are we dropping you off at your gal's doorstep?" Roscoe asked, taking up the reins. Poppy climbed up onto the wagon seat, squeezing in beside Edwood. She'd thought of nothing but Forsythia all day, but right now she had something else on her mind.

"I'll see her tomorrow," she said, beaming at the two of them. "How about we grab a drink at the saloon. Just the three of us, like old times?"

"One last time?" Edwood grimaced, looking away from her.

She threw her arms around his neck, pressing her cheek to his. "I'm not leaving you, Ed. Not really."

"But you *are* staying with her, ain't you?" Roscoe asked, a tiny note of worry in his cocky voice. That took her by surprise.

She let Edwood go and looked at them, the concern written all over their faces. "I am," she said. "At least for now. If she'll have me. But you know that doesn't mean I won't see you two again. Our paths will always cross, no matter what."

"You promise?" Roscoe said.

"I promise," she said, pulling them both into a hug. "I don't know where I'd be without you two."

She held them a moment longer before Edwood pushed them both back.

"Enough touchy-feely stuff," he scolded. "Let's go get that drink, before this gets all sappy like one of those books of yours."

Poppy laughed and they started back towards town, back to the place she hoped to one day call home, where Forsythia was tucked up in her bed asleep, with no idea that tomorrow she'd find out just how close her dreams were to coming true.

ABOUT THE AUTHOR

Rowan Dale is a nonbinary and bisexual author based on Kaurna country. They write fantasy and romance with an emphasis on queer joy and found families. They are currently working on a collaborative romantasy novel with their best friend, as well as a solo fantasy novel about bushrangers and one very underqualified, and slightly demonic, parole officer.

You can find out more about their works-in-progress and what they are reading on Instagram: @rowandaleauthor

Love, Why Do You Follow?

Leanbh Pearson

Morocco. The air is heavy with jasmine, dust and spices. Darkness clings close to our stone dwelling and the shouts of sellers in the market echo in the night. We're out on the rooftop, beneath the stars and moonlight. Charles is stretched out on the daybed, languidly swirling the wine in his goblet. My lips curve to a smile and I reach for him, our fingers entwine. I can't help it, the touch of his skin against mine is electrifying even as he stares longingly at Raquel.

Her back is to us. She's gazing over the vibrant city below. The fire-twirlers and dancers in the markets always catch her attention. Charles bends toward me our lips are gentle against each other. Still, he wants another. It's clear that he loves Raquel more than me. But we are both so deeply in love with her. There's something intoxicating about her. I can't identify it. Our kiss deepens, and Charles shifts closer wrapping his arms around my shoulders. My fingertips are soon tangled in his hazel hair.

Our lips part and I glance to our lover silhouetted against the cityscape.

"Raquel," I murmur.

She turns as if she's been waiting for us to call to her. In moments she's kneeling beside me, and her lips are on mine. We kiss with a fever intensity then breathe out against each other, our foreheads touching. The air surrounding her is fragrant with jasmine. Charles reaches from the daybed, his hand finding hers, and I step away from them. Soon, they're a tangle of limbs and hot kisses. I stride to the other side of the rooftop. We were happy once. All together. But love is a fickle thing: I realise they love each other more than either loved me but to part with Raquel and Charles is unthinkable.

I glance once more at my lovers, now partly clothed and embracing each other. Tonight, I will sleep alone. I leave them to their privacy and follow the stone staircase down the side of the house. The intense blend of spices on my tongue draws me toward the markets like a beacon and I pursue my hunger for the thrill and the unknown.

War is coming. Or so we hear. There's no sign of it amid the laughter and celebrations outside. It is the Winter Solstice and all of Morrocco's inhabitants are on the streets or celebrating at gatherings in houses. It doesn't matter; people still spill outdoors and small fireworks spark light into the night. It's time to banish the darkness even on the eve of war.

At first, I don't notice the shift the surrounding crowds. My stride is long and determined, even if I have no destination in mind. I want to be a stranger in Morrocco tonight and disappear among the throng of its citizens. Fireworks are all around me and then real fire. I stop.

The mosque ahead of me is ablaze with tongues of red and yellow flames reaching like dragons into the night. There's shouting and screaming. The crowd is flowing past me as if I am a boulder in the middle of a river. They part and keep running, yelling warnings and women wailing as they flee. Escaping from what?

Soldiers step from between the crumbling pillars of the mosque. Their swords are red, reflecting flame and glowing with a hatred I don't understand. Is this war? Has it finally reached us? I glance quickly behind me, back towards the house where I'd left Charles and Raquel. Fire has spread across the rooftops of buildings and armed men are everywhere I look. The shouting of celebration has turned to fear and now fighting is all around me.

I turn away from the ruined mosque. I'm not defenceless in this city, but I'm no match for trained soldier either. I slip the long dagger from the sheath in my boot. The weight of the weapon is a comfort in my hand. Sweat runs from my brow and drips from the hair of my fringe. It's abominably hot now. Fires have engulfed a large part of the city. I must reach Charles and Raquel.

I run, lengthening my stride as I cover the ground of cobbled streets and discarded purchases and much of Morrocco is burning. Shouts and commands from soldiers behind me. I ignore them. I keep running through the fiery night, the smoke harsh in my mouth.

I'm within a few strides of our house when a soldier steps from the fire. I skid to a halt. Flames reflect on the metallic surface of his armour and my dagger feels useless against the broadsword he holds. Before I can strike, strong hands grab my arms, pinning them to my side. The dagger clatters to the cobblestones.

Soldiers swarm the house and Charles is shouting. Raquel screams and the sound ricochets through me like a bolt of lightning. I must get to her. She's in danger. Of all of us, Raquel never trained to fight. She's not got a warrior's spirit. Charles is a tall figure on the rooftop, obscured by smoke and the number of soldiers subduing him. But it's Raquel I see clearly. She's backed away from the fighting and stands with her heels precariously balanced on the edge of the roof.

Time stills and there is no sound, no colour to the night anymore. I watch the inevitable happen. Raquel rears back from a soldier reaching for her. Her nightgown is unbuttoned, and the sheer nightdress flows in a breeze I don't feel. I'm numb. I can only stare as she tips backwards and falls. She's a cascade of rich fabrics and flowing hair. The scent of jasmine reaches me: the only piece of her I will ever know again.

Her head hits the cobblestones below with a bone-shattering noise I try to block from my mind. She must be dead. This can't happen. I struggle against the soldiers, but they hold me firm. Someone makes a comment, and they laugh. On the rooftop, Charles is screaming and screaming her name. Raquel. I can only stare at her broken and ruined body. My love. Our love is gone.

#

I stepped over the broken wall; chunks of stone and mortar scattered around like fallen giants. The cannon blast had ripped apart the fortifications on this side of the castle. Ahead, a pathway went to the bridge, the cobblestones now cracked and chipped. The sky above me is an angry burnt orange. Between the ruined castle and the expanse of the battlefield is where I might find him. But first was the wood. It was haunted long before armies ravaged the land and the more blood that seeped into those roots only twisted it further. Still, I must venture there to find him. My Charles.

Movement on the periphery of my eye. I turned. Was it her? She never showed herself, but the hairs raised on the back of my neck. Nothing now but ash swirling to the ground. She'd been there. If I tried, I could sense the light perfume of jasmine. Those heady days of love, lust, and youth: humid nights bathed in moonlight and the air scented with jasmine. The three of us were inseparable. Then war had come and the maelstrom of destruction and taken her from Charles and me. Did she follow him as she did me?

I had to find Charles. The castle behind me was nothing more than ruins, the battlements like broken teeth. I moved carefully along the shattered road to the collapsed portcullis, which now sagged over the drawbridge. I'd escaped the worst of the fighting in the Keep, a maze of confusion and death.

A hot wind blew into my face, carrying the rotten scent of the battle ahead. I ground my teeth and walked the broken trail that left the castle and went into the woods. Ancient magic had blighted the wood, and nothing grew there now but twisted things. Still, the bridge was on the far side and many a foolish one had taken axes or flames to the cursed trees trying to find a way through. Ill fortune had befallen them all.

My boots scuffed the cracked cobbles, and I prayed to God I'd pass safely beneath this canopy. I stepped under the naked branches of the wood, and, to my surprise, the trees were scarred and scorched. Fire had raged through here before the army followed behind. Those bare branches stood stark against the sky like pikes. I'd crossed many battlefields, but these woods chilled my marrow. Darkness dwelled here.

I pulled the grey hood over my hair. Sweat ran freely between my shoulder blades, but the weight of my cloak was a familiar comfort. An acrid wind gusted through the forest, twisting the length of the cloak around my legs. I shifted it aside to keep my hand on the pommel of my sword.

My feet walked the road, but my eyes roamed the surrounding woods. Bodies hung from trees, forms blackened and bloated. These were the horrors committed in the name of war. Who were these unfortunate wretches strung up by the enemy? Who were they to deserve such a horrendous fate? The ropes groaned beneath their terrible burdens as the dead soldiers swung in the wind.

"Elspeth."

I sensed her proximity; my body's instincts alerting me to her presence behind. I ignored the creeping unease and pushed forward, fingers tapping anxiously on my sword hilt.

"Elspeth."

"Raquel?"

Cruel laughter on the breeze circled me from every direction. It wasn't her, couldn't be her. We'd had our lover's tiffs and fights between the three of us, but she'd never been so cold to me.

"Elspeth."

It was *her* voice. I couldn't deny that. Oh, how I'd missed the sound of her. I stepped from the path, ankle-deep in smoke rising from the charred ground. She'd haunted me these years and never once answered my pleas. Why had she chosen now? Her presence was surrounding me, chiding me. I'd strayed deep into the woods and severed branches snagged my feet trying to trip me. Her melodious laughter echoed through the woods, but there was a harsher lilt to it than I remembered.

"Raquel?"

I stood in a hollow. Bodies hung from every tree around me, the skin blistered and flesh raw beneath. Everywhere I looked, there were these terrible offerings. Why would Raquel lead me here?

A wraith manifested from the waist-high smoke. It was female with long dark hair and green eyes but bore no other similarity to my Raquel. I still felt her behind me, strength and support when I needed her most. I drew the blade at my hip. Mist clung to my legs, stretching upward like hands reaching from the earth.

"You're not her," I snarled.

The wraith hissed, baring elongated canines. It moved fast across the ground. I stepped forward, bringing up my blade. A silver shimmer of runes ran along the steel, and it cut through the darkness which had forged the mockery of my Raquel. The wraith screamed in rage, its fanged mouth open, black eyes boring into mine. Another sweep of my sword took it through the chest, slicing the fabric of its being apart. It hissed and dissipated into the smoke that had formed it. It wasn't destroyed. Such evils can't be so easily vanquished, but it was gone for now. The silent dead surrounded me, twisting on their ropes in reminder that war's another evil made by humans.

I sheathed my blade. I couldn't look at hanged men and women in the woods. My stomach churned with revulsion at my own cowardice. War was all anyone experienced anymore, and I was as guilty of savagery as the next man or woman. I fled the woods, boots raising ash from burned leaves on the forest floor. I stumbled onto the road and towards the stone arches of the bridge.

It had once been a magnificent bridge spanning the river which rushed with deafening ferocity below. The impressive black pillars had toppled into the gorge and more evidence of where siege weapons had destroyed much of the structure, leaving a mere spindle of black rock crossing the gulf of the gorge with pitch-dark water below. A sharp, unpleasant odour lifted from the river, a foulness that stung my eyes. Wiping away unintentional tears, I moved back from the edge. Opposing armies had twice-poisoned the mountain springs near their enemy's camps and now even the greatest of our rivers flowed with nothing but bitter liquid.

The air stirred behind me, and I knew she was close. Was Raquel urging me onwards? Towards Charles? Beyond the gorge and over the next rise, would I find the battlefield and my Charles?

I stepped cautiously onto the bridge. The large stone slabs were cracked from the destruction wrought by siege weapons. I could only hope it was safe to cross. My blade was unsheathed at my side and edging forward, boots kicking up shards of black rock. Below, the river roared with the promise of death and reeked from the foul toxins within. I stared straight ahead, one boot before the other. In the middle of the spindly bridge, the roar of the river, I heard voices of the dead, a clamour that rolled like thunder up from the gorge. It wasn't only the woods that were haunted. Wherever blood was spilled on the earth, the restless dead called for attention.

Sweat ran down my back, but the cool touch of ghostly fingertips on my cheek kept me grounded. Legs trembling with the painstaking effort of crossing the narrow ledge of stone, I staggered to the opposite side. Half- falling, I grabbed for the broken pillars to steady myself.

A twisted hedge of metal spikes passed along the top of the ridge ahead of me marking the battlefield. Severed heads were arrayed upon the iron pikes, sightless orbits staring at me. discernible as human. I straightened, lifting my sword and moved toward the awaiting terrors.

A wasteland stretched as far as I could see. Standards of the armies were splintered and shattered in the mud. Blood drenched the soil, more than could ever be washed away by rain.

What dark crop would blossom from so much death and sorrow?

"Raquel? We must find Charles."

I hoped my words would reach her. She'd haunted my days and nights, a spectre of my dreams and nightmares. I knew Raquel always loved Charles more than me, and I'd accepted that long ago. Still, I didn't know why she followed me so relentlessly.

I stepped onto the battlefield; muddy earth soaked with blood and gore. Searching the standards planted in the ground, I looked for the only one I wanted to find, but the fabrics were tattered, gore-splattered and barely recognisable. I proceeded deliberately through the aftermath of the battle, setting my feet carefully among charred bodies around me, no long recognizable as human. A team of horses and cannons were a tangled wreckage of broken limbs and wheels. Flocks of carrion birds wheeled about the wasteland, a chorus of harsh voices singing for the battle's dead.

Sword in hand, I strode over the battleground like death moving over our countries. Ashes clung to my clothing; soot stained my face as I searched from one pile of bodies to the next. I stooped over a knight, his armour plating broken by the force of a battle axe. Dead, all dead. I was alone. Straightening, I looked behind me, seeking that familiar presence of Raquel's ghost. She had gone. Cold sweat trickled down my spine. I was truly alone.

I stumbled across the muddy ground, tripping over bodies and body parts. Fear drove me up a slope. Since the beginning of the war, I'd never been alone. I slowed, squinting against the orange haze of the sky. There! The battle standard I was searching for: a golden moon cast against a blue sky. It was torn and muddied, set crookedly in the ground.

I found him beside it. Charles lay with his sword and shield broken. His warhorse had fallen, the weight of the dead stallion now crushing him into the corpses and mud beneath him. Heedless of the piled dead under my feet, I stumbled to him. Kneeling at his side, I gently removed the helm, covering his head and face. His skin was grey as though the life had already leeched from him.

"Charles."

"Do you think of her?"

"Raquel? I've felt her presence ever since she died."

"Me too."

I brushed the sweaty hair from his brow. "She's here now, behind you."

Charles's focus slipped from my face and over my left shoulder. I turned but could see nothing, though I was sure her ghost was nearby. I caressed his cheek and listened to the ugly rattle of his breathing. We'd been closer than any three could be. It'd been a fierce love, one that united and broke us apart. I'd not begrudged Charles and Raquel their passion. I'd always known he loved her more than me.

Now the shadow of Death stretched across the battlefield, darkening the wasteland, and reached for Charles. I held him in my arms as his last breath sighed from his lungs. Tears tracked through my ash-stained cheeks. The familiar presence of Raquel lingered a moment behind me before she, too, departed.

I sat back on my heels in the middle of the war-ravaged land. I was truly alone for the first time since the three of us had met. Raquel gone long ago. Charles now taken from me by war. Where will my path take me now?

ABOUT THE AUTHOR

Leanbh Pearson (Any) lives on Ngunnawal Country in Canberra, Australia. An award-winning LGBTQ and disability author of horror and dark fantasy inspired by folklore, fairytales, myth, history and climate. Leanbh's judged numerous awards, an invited panelist and avid book reviewer. Leanbh has been awarded ASA, AHWA and HWA mentorships and 2023 HWA Diversity Grant. Leanbh's alter-ego is an academic in archaeology, evolution and prehistory. A museum devotee, insomniac and photography enthusiast, Leanbh is always aided by canine assistants.

https://linktr.ee/leanbhpearson

Kookaburra Cruel

Aaron Dries

Down by the river watching water sleek by. Ripples feel predetermined, as if everything was meant to flow this way, and no other. It confirms what I already know. I'm meant to be here, on this day, dodging wombat shit, watched by preppy kangaroos that grunt in my direction before bouncing into the scrub. I finger the gun in my raincoat pocket. It's April 11, 1991.

And I'm scouting for the perfect place to blow my brains out.

Picture my blood running in the snake belly black water after I pull the trigger. See the snails tic-tac-toeing my cheeks with slime where my body fell by the riverbank. Twigs in my hair. Spiders crawl from burrows in the earth to hide under my shirt. I see all this, and more. So clear. But then the corpse opens its eyes and sits up to look at me, brain oozing from the bullet hole, down its cheeks, between its lips. Snails stick to its skin, wet eyes googling.

"Are you sure you want to do this, Detective?" it says, gurgling on grey matter.

"I'm not a detective anymore," I imagine myself saying. "And you know it."

"Chantal. . ." The corpse sounds like my mother—not that I've heard her voice in years. Time is a thief. The resemblance is in the schooling, in how small it makes me feel. *"If you're doing this to be with Matthew, know this: he isn't here with us. Not as you remember him, anyway."*

I slip my hand into my pocket where the gun barrel is icy to the touch. Shaking. Kookaburras laugh at my lack of conviction, at the cliché I've become. Rain patters my coat, drums the leaves. Thoughts no longer align—they are torn things that sting when re-wired into order. A pulse in every inch of me. My heart is trying to convince me I'm whole, still alive. That I have a choice here.

My finger on the trigger loosens.

Kookaburras cackle louder. Three share a branch in a nearby tree. A gutted snake dangles from one of their beaks, the flesh pink as rosewater. They laugh again to let me know this is their territory. My body will be theirs to claim should I die out here. Don't look to the kookaburra for sympathy, no matter the warmth of its laugh.

"No, not yet then," I say aloud, and look back to my corpse.

Relieved, it nods and reclines on the mud. She looks comfortable. Grass grows up through her skin, which is sun-spotted from too many years doing grunt work on the beat, knitting her in green until she's no longer there. Just a mound of nature for the wombats to dig up later. Flowers bloom on her chest, petals opening to free pollen-streaked spiders.

"Soon, though."

I head up the hill to the cabin. My legs are heavy. Everything is heavy. It's dusk. Kookaburras call after me but I don't look back.

#

Dooling, the owner who lives on the other side of the huge property, has left a basket on the doorstep. I hadn't locked up before heading to the river. Doing so didn't make sense. I wonder if Dooling came inside when I was out, if he snooped. Distrust is an old cop reflex. Given the chance, I would have snooped, too. It's in my nature to pry where I'm not wanted. The ability to do so without being noticed was what made me good at my job.

Step over the basket. Draw the sliding glass door open. Stick my head into the small room.

It doesn't *feel* different inside.

Strangers dislodge the puzzle pieces of a space without noticing. They shift air and shadows, indications of where they have been, and if you look hard enough, what they did within that space presents itself. And why. Out of whack shadows. A scent where there was no scent before. The condensation ring on the tabletop that's one inch to the right of the glass. Strangers get carried away and overlook details that incriminate them later.

Cabin shadows are where they should be. Everything smells the same, just danker. The glass hasn't moved.

My body starts to unclench.

Suspicion comes easy to people like me. Considering the cases I've worked, I don't run myself over hot coals for this. My ex-husband did that enough for the both of us.

I retrieve the picnic basket, knees popping as I bend. Mum had Arthritis, too. All the women in my family had it. I'm the last now. A note is tucked between a loaf of bread wrapped in a tea towel, and a bottle of red wine.

Sorry, Chantal. Ran out of time to bring this down earlier. You were out. There's a bottle opener in the bottom drawer to the left of the sink. Bread is homemade. You should have everything you need to enjoy your stay. I don't imagine our paths will cross. Leave the key under the doormat on checkout. All the best, Dooling.

I read between the lines. What's there is evident. Some things I add.

Don't worry about me dropping by again. You don't want to see me, and I don't want to see you. It's like I'm not even here, Chantal. This is a transaction. For all intents and purposes, you're alone way out here in the scrub. A million miles away from anyone, really. And if the wind is blowing away from the homestead, or if there's thunder. . .

. . . I won't hear the bullet at all.

Wind pushes eucalyptus leaves into circles on the veranda, tightening circles. Gumnuts bounce on the wooden boards. A chill climbs my back. I step into the cabin I rented on a whim because my home in Canberra has become a poisonous place. Yank the door shut. The basket is lighter than expected—or maybe I'm stronger than I give myself credit for. Look back through the glass. The vegetation is thick with veiny branches. Faces in the tree trunks all sad or screamy. Flickers of gloomy sky like scratches on an old skillet after too much scrubbing.

The thought of food makes me ill, so I pour myself a gin and diet ginger ale instead. Dooling's wine can wait. It's almost five thirty. My toiletries bag is on the counter with my lipstick and foundation inside, the clamshell mirror I look at only when I must because I hate what I see. Hiking boots smothered in mud by the door. I'm sure it won't be long until I'm back in them and wandering outside. These walls are closing in again. There's the book I brought out of habit. No television. No radio. The clothes in my suitcase are all too big. The past year has taken a toll on my body. I'm fifty-six but look older. Police work does that. I'm hardened but had hoped I'd still be of use to someone. Nobody wants me. Nobody calls. This woman here is tainted goods. Her son is dead. Husband run off. What good is the gold retirement watch if there's nobody around to ask her the time anymore?

Another drink. It burns all the way down. Good.

You deserve to burn.

The rental is nice, just small. It's all I need. The perfect place to suicide. I don't want to do it in my house. I've spent too many years keeping the floors clean just to flood the place with gore. I'm being glib but sue me. I don't want to die in the house I shared with my men.

The cabin is neutral ground. I've always loved the mountains.

Bogong moths the size of mice tap at the window trying to get in at the lamps. I feel their kamikaze strikes against the glass in my shins, in my tooth fillings. I hate them. The fluttering of their wings reminds me of how we kids used to peg playing cards to the spokes of bikes and the sound they made as we rode. *Fft-fft-fft-fft-fft.* My bike riding years are behind me. And most of my friends are gone.

I don't eat. Consider killing myself again. Think, no, not tonight. I'm too annoyed by the moths at the windows. I came up here to feel calm and they've got me agitated. I decide to go to bed instead. It's early but who cares. What is time to someone like me? Time is a punchline and I'm the joke leading up to it.

The mattress is in the corner of the cabin to the right of the front door. I flip back the blanket and hear something strike the floor. It isn't loud. It doesn't seem heavy. It isn't one of my things. It is alien.

A silver earring sits on the hardwood floor. It's small, delicate, almost handsome in design. At first, I think it's the shape of a star. Reach down. Pick it up. Turn it over in my hand. No, it's a starfish. The corners are curled, as though propelling itself through water, against the channels and currents of my palm wrinkles. The hook is thin, clean. It snatches light from the bedside lamp and glimmers. I roll the earring between my thumb and forefinger, wondering who it belonged to, and make a mental note to pop it in an envelope for Dooling or the cleaner, whoever finds my body.

Hi there. Found this earring. Could be yours or maybe it belongs to the last person to rent the place. Hope you find the owner. It's a pretty thing. All the best, Chantal.

PS: sorry about the mess! Hope you're insured. Those stains are going to be a real bitch to get out of your curtains.

I place the earring on the bedside table and take a swill of water from the glass I'd left there. Soon my reflux will kick in. It always does after heavy drinking. Ease off my readers and turn off the light to study the ceiling in the dark. Memories creep in on cue.

#

Matthew has been dead for two-and-a-half years. My husband left me eight months ago.

I've had time to process Neville's abrupt departure. But I will never recover from the loss of my son. He saved me once. At the time, everyone told me suicide is murder—Neville, my colleagues at the department. They saw I'd had reasons to do it, means to do it, and had set aside the time. Nothing else mattered to them. Everyone except Matthew.

"Mum, what are you *doing*?" he cried when he came into my bedroom and found me on the bed. He'd later tell me he came over because his father was away for work, and he knew I'd been put on stress leave. I hadn't answered the phone in two days.

"No-no-no-NO-NO!"

I was awake enough to feel shame. Shame is a physical hurt in the flesh. Coloured pills and the numb forever the CAUTION labels promised didn't come through, empty as an 'I do'. Cut to the vomit when they pumped my stomach in the ambulance. I wanted out of this world at forty-seven, and somehow found myself alive with my adult son in the back of an ambulance instead.

"It's okay, Mum," I remember him saying.

"Sorry. So sorry. Sorry. . ."

"You're going to be okay."

There are other memories from those following days, all equally acute. Neville walking into the room where I was being treated and the bird-like way he perched on the mattress beside me. His red eyes. His red nose. His red capillaries. "Christ, Chantal. How could you be so stupid." It wasn't a question. He lifted his head, biting his thin red lower lip. Just one more word to silence me.

"Selfish."

That night in the hospital, I looked at the white walls and saw Amanda Lu.

She was the sister of the girl who had been murdered a year before I went to the medicine cabinet seeking bottles with warnings stickers. Amanda died because I didn't pick up on certain clues. She was murdered like her sister. Their killer stabbed them both forty-three times, cut off her hands and feet. I know the bastard's name but don't say it, hardly ever think it. My mind is a carousel of victims. Every face is remembered. It's my way of honouring who they were, not how they looked on the slab. With Amanda's assistance, we were closing in on our prime suspect. But he got to her first. I think he did it to send me a message. In a cruel cheat of fate, he was struck by a passing truck after fleeing Amanda's apartment. The knives were still on his person, as were Amanda's hands and feet. I could hardly believe it when my partner told me. It only seemed real when I saw the bastard's outline on the bitumen, chalk running in the rain. The lesson had been taught. I was—am—a failure of unforgivable magnitude.

Amanda Lu.

I couldn't save her, or her sister. And my son isn't here to save me a second time. Perhaps that is for the best.

The cabin is mine for five days. It even has a name. 'Kyle'. I saw the holiday rental advertisement in The Canberra Times classifieds. Dooling is over the hill, through a forest of pine trees, on an alpaca farm. I walked that way earlier, rain dripping through the canopy, cartoonish red and white toadstools everywhere. At a bluff, I passed between a gap in the boulders to peer at the owner's house down there in the valley. Nice place. Two storeys. Neat garden. Alpacas chewed grass in their pens. I went to the river, fingering a trigger every step of the way. My goodbyes went unheard. I no longer feared death, only pain. Pain, I'd seen up close.

The Matthew I used to know:

Handsome and tall, the spit of my father. A popular kid who grew into a sporty adult fond of a beer, and with a laugh that carried through the house when he visited from Sydney. He loved his mum, and only to me disclosed shades of the life he kept from us. Shades were enough. I didn't push my questions. I tried not to make assumptions (hard to do for most people, but harder for cops) and separated my hopes from his hopes for fear of him resenting me as he did others. He appreciated that. When Matthew looked you in the eye and smiled, you felt alive, like you had someone on your team. The dimples in his cheeks that called back to the boy he used to be. His hard, calloused hands. Workman's hands.

Versus Matthew at the end:

A skeleton wrapped in a sheet of skin with no fat or muscle between. Shitting himself. Vomiting blood. And then in the final months, the way he stared at me and didn't know who I was. Dimples stretched away. Silver rings slid onto the mattress because his fingers were so bony. In the night, he screamed the names of men I hadn't wanted to know about, and he never wanted to disclose to me. I wished I knew who these people were, and hoped they knew I would welcome them at our doorstep where I cared for him should they knock, that I would keep them safe from Neville. With time (not a lot of it, though), Matthew became less a man than a Condition with a capital C. So, when I held him and kissed his fingers, I had to acknowledge my love for The Condition. That was all that was left: the plague which seemed to target men born a certain way, men like my son. The invader that had overtaken this country of a person, burned his crops and enslaved his people. I loved The Condition, the disease, in the hopes I could gain its trust and control it. This was a foolish thing to invest effort in. One of many wasted moments.

It got to the point, alone in the house with Matthew, where I had to whisper at him to let go.

"Stop fighting, my son. You're free."

Neville must have been searching for reasons to travel. He was hardly around, especially towards the end. A queer kid had never been easy for him. But to have that queer go out because of the plague. . . *that* he couldn't handle. The diagnosis confirmed something in Neville, that he'd been right to hate all along. It got to the point where others—family, the occasional friend—were too afraid to hold our son for fear they would catch it. I held him. I kissed him. Bathed him. Mopped his shit and blood. I wore rubber gloves. Scrubbed my hands until the skin cracked. His skeleton rose through his skin as though trying to climb into the grave. Kind eyes turned black. My boy was better than this. I used to think, *what a waste*. And that's what I told him when he sat me down and said he was sick. I regret saying this. It's a foolish thing to merit time in what you don't get as opposed to what you do. I'm happy to have had what I was blessed with. Though I hungered for more—still do. His absence, the nothingness of his non-existence, is a weight in my day that will never ease. He is with Amanda Lu. I do not want their weight on me any longer. Better a flash of light and a bang. Then whatever comes next. I've never been stupid enough to believe in God. I wish I could be that easily fooled.

Moths kept trying to get in all night long.

Fft-fft. Fft-fft-fft-fft. Fft. Fft-fft-fft-fft-fft-fft.

#

Sleep must have claimed me at some point because dawn breaks and the kookaburras are laughing. Groggy, I reach for my glass of water and touch something warm and foreign on the bedside table instead. Snatch back my hand. Put on my glasses. Jolt in the bed.

"Jesus Christ!"

The earring is still there.

Only now it's threaded through the lobe of a human ear.

#

Fine hairs along the rim—if that's what you call it. The outer ear. Tiny hairs rise as though capable of sensory reaction. I place the remains (though, in all honesty, it feels more like the beginnings of something and not the leftovers) on the dining table next to the guest book and a map of walking trails. Rain announces itself on the tin-roof. I sip my tea and rub my chin, glancing from the ear to the gun I set by the toaster and Vegemite.

How truly odd this is, I think. *There really is no other way to put it.*

Odd.

Another me, maybe the married me, or the motherly me, might have been fearful of finding an ear. I'm not those people anymore. Why should the appearance of a body part shock me when parts of my body have been numbing out, bit by bit, piece by piece, for months? I am zombie, a necrotic thing. The only difference is that I carry my dead bits and pieces with me.

So, what the hell do I do with it?

The lime green landline beckons from the wall. Dooling's number is printed on a laminated card bound to the keys he left out for me the prior day. How would that conversation go?

"Uh, sorry to bother you, but did you happen to leave a magic earring in the cabin? It seems to have grown an ear overnight. Do you, uh, want to come down here and take care of it for me? I've got enough on my plate. Thanks!"

Maybe I should flush it down the toilet, as I did one of Matthew's dead canaries when he was a kid. The bird died while he was at school. Neville and I told our son that Nero got out of his cage and flew home to be with the other canaries. There were hundreds, even thousands of them in the sky, calling out to him. And Nero listened. It wasn't anyone's fault.

"But how did Nero open the cage from the inside? Nero doesn't have hands!"

Smart kid. Always was.

"I think something happened to Nero, and you and Dad don't want to tell me because you're worried about how it'll make me feel," he'd said with tears in his eyes, sounding so even-tempered and adult it aged me years within a second. "Well, I'm sad. I'm just really, really sad."

Sighing, I place the ear on the table. Leave it there. Pick up my umbrella. Climb inside my raincoat. Put the gun in the pocket. Take to the hills to think— and maybe more. I don't lock up. There's nothing in the cabin worth stealing because I value nothing. There are crows in the sky. Sparrows here and there. No canaries.

I come home five hours later to find that the ear has grown a head.

\#

It blinks, mouthing words yet unable to speak, having no lungs with which to breathe, no throat to muscle out the noise. The head tongues the roof of its dry mouth. I go to the fridge by the sink and wrestle an ice cube out of the tray. Offer it to the head, and when he blinks twice at me, tongue extending, I slide it into his mouth. It sucks for a bit and then crushes the cube between its jaws.

"Don't chew!" I say, extending a hand. "You'll hurt your—" The hand stills. "Teeth." Drops. Jaws no longer grind. I grip my rising and falling chest. Every inch of my body is vulnerable. Exposed. This is who I really am. I am a mother who hungers for someone to parent. And this thing on the counter now has me by the short and curlies.

No, not a thing. This is a man.

He's younger than Matthew when he died, maybe twenty-three, twenty-four. Caucasian. Handsome. Sad, skittish deer eyes. Sallow cheeks. Lips like a Roman statue.

I'm not sure how long I sit and stare. Long enough for the light to change. Fatigue settles in. Emotions I can't name niggle with a hundred tiny mouths, but not even this is enough through the wall of numbness. Not yet. It's good to feel something. It might be shock, but sleep is something I need above all else. Unfortunately, I always wake. Cops never die in their sleep. That's just the way it goes.

I can't have the head looking at me while I nap (I might be far gone but I'm not immune to the creep factor), so I roll the head over. "Sorry," I say, touching it gingerly—all fingertips, no palms. The mass of meat faces the microwave and Dooling's basket. I run my fingers through the man's duckish hair. Should he have lived to be in his forties, I imagine he may have been bald. He's warm.

Who are his parents? Do they know what became of him? How would his mother feel knowing he's here with me?

I lay my head against the pillow.

#

My eyes bolt open at a voice within the room.

There are still a few hours of light left in the day. I squint against the glare that has crept through the port hole in the slanted ceiling, stalking the floor and onto the bed. I haven't moved, and my bones grind as I lift myself up off the mattress.

The head has grown half a torso.

"Okay," I say. Take a breath. "Here we go."

Rubbery lungs inflate and deflate beneath the man's broad shoulders. Veins slither across the tabletop, slow roots in search of soil. Flesh glimmers around the edges as it crystalises and then grows lax, undulating, each flex expanding outwards in new growths, a tide of meat drawing closer to shore with every wave. And I'm that shore. It's me he wants.

"You're awake," the man says, voice a rasp. *"Please, lady, you're in danger."*

"W-what?"

"Turn me over so I can see you."

You don't attend as many crime scenes as I have without developing the gall to handle a John or Jane Doe. I scuttle off the bed, go to the table, and take the chunk of man by the shoulders. My grip is tenacious, more *me*, this time. Roll him over so he's earring side up. He's feverish. Bright blue eyes peer into me.

"Thank you," says the man.

"You're, um, welcome."

"Can I have another ice-cube?"

I oblige him. "You said I was in danger?"

The man pushes the ice from one side of his mouth to the other. Hot breath over the cold cube makes his words steam. *"What day is it?"* he asks. *"What date?"*

"April twelfth."

The man blinks. Tears in the corner of his eyes. He prepares to speak, maybe taking a moment to absorb where he is and what has become of him.

"I was killed five days ago." His brow furrows. Confusion muscles into a frightened kind of hope. *"That means my friend might still be alive."*

Now is as good a time as any to take a seat. I'm light-headed. My hands interlink on the table. Gears shift. My detective voice kicks in. "What's your name, son?"

"Scotty."

It's as if in saying his name, acknowledging who he used to be, the man has given himself permission to cry. Tears appear silver in the cool light. His loss is confirmed for both of us now.

"Scotty McLain. I'm from Canberra. I came to this cabin with my friend. We were asleep when someone came through the door in the night. We're in the middle of nowhere, we didn't think we needed to lock up. The bastard got in when we were sleeping."

Something in me thaws. I think of the cases I didn't solve, the wrongs I didn't right. Amanda Lu and her sister and how their body bags protruded at all the wrong angles in the morgue. All those closed casket funerals I watched at a cop's distance, where you appear to be paying respects but are scanning the mourners for suspects because killers are compulsive creatures who feed off suffering. The situation facing me now isn't about whether I believe the man or not. Rather, if I still believe in my own abilities. Perhaps this is a test. But who—I can't help wondering—is the teacher?

"The intruder. Who was this man?" I ask.

"It's the owner," Scotty says, quick as thunder close to the strike. *"Burly fella. Sickly looking, but stronger. He's so tall. Like a giant. His name's Dooling."*

My mind leapfrogs to the note in the basket. The neat handwriting—careful, considerate, swishes and flicks.

"How do I know you're telling me the truth, Scotty?"

"I . . ."

My eyebrow raises. I need to challenge him. Need to know.

"I can prove it."

Scotty closes his blue eyes, which are so like Matthew's. There's that same sympathy in them, a fish out of its bowl *I-can't-believe-this-is-happening-to-me* naiveté. It's enough to make me burst. *I don't want this. This isn't how things are meant to go.* Numbness is what I need, numbness more than anything because numb is safe.

"Oh, you can prove it, can you?"

I'm laughing. The sound has a kookaburra cruelty to it. I hate myself.

The dead man nods, so much as he can nod, right temple against the tablecloth. He shivers and coughs. His mouth opens. Eyes pinch. My pulse quickens with expectancy, a feeling that everything is slipping off keel.

Scotty regurgitates up a human pinkie finger. It flops on the table beside his mouth, webbed in greenish strands of saliva. The second knuckle is tattooed with the letter E.

I stumble backwards. "Fucking hell!"

Scotty clears his throat. *"He's only got four fingers left on his right hand."* His voice is clearer now. *"I bit this one off when he attacked me. I swallowed it whole."*

Bile slips up my throat and I swallow it down. There's a part of me that wants to dive to the raincoat by the door, pull the gun out, shove the barrel in my mouth and do what I came here to do. I'm not doing that, though. I don't know *why* I'm not doing that.

Scotty speaks again.

"Don't," I say. "Don't—"

"Matthew was wrong."

"Shhh."

"When things were really bad, when you were caring for him at the end, he told you he was afraid there was nothing. . . beyond."

"I don't want to hear it!" I cover my ears. Scotty's words cut through. My stomach turns again, nerves in riot. The arthritic pain twists and clenches and splints in elbows and knees and shoulders. It's everywhere.

"If only there was. . . only the pit."

I glare at the man on the table. In his eyes, I see refractions of light cast from some other place. My ticket to that place is in the chamber of the gun. That light is both cold and hot at once, and I hate that my son—that all sons and daughters—are lit by it in the end.

"There is no love in the beyond, Chantal," Scotty tells me. I hear the mourning in him. *"Where there was love there are only cogs. And we all turn. We all have a place. Cogs on cogs on cogs, all of us powering the machine. Powering It. We all turn."*

"You can't tell me this, Scotty. You can't. It's not right."

"I escaped, but they'll know I'm gone soon."

"Close your mouth."

"Help me, Chantal. While there's still time. I can hear them turning."

\#

Gin burns all the way down. The muddy boots are tight about my ankles. I set off for the house on the other side of the hill, through the boulders, across the valley. The folds of the rubber slicker wisp as I march over uneven earth, crushing mushrooms.

The image of the severed finger with the letter E tattooed on its knuckle probes my brain. It knows my will is squishy. It knows that it is *inside* me now, and the only way to purge it is to see this through.

It's four thirty in the afternoon. Evening will fall soon. There's hardly twilight at this time of the year. Night eats day and then we live in its belly until it shits us out again. We endure this over and over, and each time we wake, there's a little less of us left. This is what it is to get old. I know I was—no, *am*—right to want no more of that cycle.

That little slip into past tense makes me uncomfortable.

The *was.*

Do I stop every so often to reconsider my decision to pursue this? You bet. But my legs keep moving, step after step, a beat in search of beat, my body, my soul, and my need for answers. Even here at the end of who I used to be, I still have to know. Because I've been faced with a mystery. I sense the mystery as to why Scotty came to me is old and cosmic. Within that mystery lies a secret. And secrets are man-made.

According to Scotty, the man on the property did the worst thing a man can do.

So, detect, Detective.

I peer over the ridge. It would take me half-an-hour to reach the house below. All going to plan (ha—what plan?), I'd be trekking back to my cabin well after dark. There would be no light with the clouds as thick as they were in the mountains. I sit on one of the rocks and shake my head. Of all the cabins I could have rented, it had to be Dooling's.

The kookaburras are laughing again.

#

"Hey there, mate," I say to the enormous man bent over in the garden. He also wears a slicker, only his is garbage bag green. The rain has petered off. Just little spits every now and then. The garden would be soft. A perfect time to turn blood and bone. Alpacas bray in my direction, their pelts knotted and slimy with oil and water.

I hold my ground.

Dooling stands and faces me. Scotty was correct. The owner is a giant of a kind. Easily seven feet of bulk, a mixture of muscle and fat. A moon of a creature. He wears heavy duty gardening gloves on both hands, gripping a three-pronged trowel in his right—it looks comically small compared to the rest of him.

"You're the lady in the cabin, yeah?" he says. His voice is buttery.

"Chantal."

"That's right."

"And you're Mister Dooling?"

"Just Dooling," he says, nodding. His eyes are small and round in his face. I hear him breathing from where I stand, half a dozen yards away, the space between us full of sun-bleached pinwheels stabbed into the grass. There is mucus in his throat. It rattles. I want to cough for him.

"I'm just out walking, Dooling."

"Weather for the ducks," he says, gesturing to the sky. It spits again in reply.

"I was wondering if you could help me with something?"

Another phlegmy inhale, followed by the rattle of breath fighting its way from his thick throat. The air we share vibrates in his presence, with the exertion it takes for him to keep living. His stormy energy. I'm afraid of him. The numbness has receded now. Coming here was a mistake. I wonder if he can taste my motive on the wind. If he's who I think he is, what he is, he already knows I've come to cause him grief.

"You should have used the phone in your cabin," he says. The crown of his bald head is sweaty—or maybe it's just from the rain. "Whatever you needed, I could've arranged and saved you a walk."

Alpacas stir. A crow calls.

The pinwheels are turning, turning.

"You know," he continues. "Brought you whatever you need. Even if it was after dark. I've got a torch."

I wonder if, five days earlier, in the dark, that same torch illuminated the earth between his house and the cabin he rents in The Canberra Times classified section. I believe it did. I believe he turned the torch off before stepping into the clearing. I believe he waited for Scotty and his friend to turn off the lights. And I believe Dooling waited a while, out in the trees, until it seemed the right amount of time for a person to fall asleep. I believe he could have waited longer, just to be sure, only Dooling couldn't wait. He is impatient. His boots would have crushed the dewy grass as he stepped closer to the cabin, that his heaviness would have made the veranda floorboards creak. This sound would have alerted Scotty. And the end would have come fast and blunt. I believe Dooling may have put the torch in his huge mouth, the plastic tight between his teeth, to light the way back through the trees, across the valley, as he dragged Scotty's friend home. I believe that it would have been after dawn by the time Dooling got back to clean the mess he made in the cabin. Scotty was buried in sunlight. But by that time, Scotty was in the beyond. He was turning.

We all turn, Scotty told me. And even though I didn't want to believe that, too, I did.

"I'm sure you do have a torch," I say. "I didn't think. I'm a feet-first kind of gal."

Dooling studies me. "How old are you? No spring chicken. Sorry, I don't mean to be rude. I'd hate for someone like you to fall, is all. There's lots of foxholes. Roll an ankle in weather like this, I might never have heard your calls."

I look at his hands again. Five fingered gloves on each.

"I'm a widow," I lie. Well, sort-of lie. This is an indication of age, or at least as much rope as I am willing to gift him.

"A widow."

"Yeah."

The man drops his guard. "Me too. House sure feels empty without the ole girl around no more."

"Sorry to hear," I say.

"So, what is it?"

"What's what?"

"What do you need?"

"Oh," I say. "Sugar. Can't have my coffee without it. When I was younger, I'd never have a cuppa this late in the day. But you don't need as much sleep when you're older."

"There's sugar in your cabin right above the—"

"Ants."

"What?"

"Ants got to it. Little buggers."

"Damn things. I'll have to spray the place again."

The wind picks up, making the alpacas cry. It sounds like a warning—not that I need one. Rain comes down harder, sluicing Dooling's oily face. He is a golem of a thing, an assembly of parts, all different sizes. His trowel is like a third, arthritic hand that reminds me of Mum at the end. How she held me even though it hurt to hold me.

Where there was love there are cogs.

"I'll get you some sugar," he says, limping towards the front door of the double storey house. I follow close behind, but not too close. A safe distance. Though, from my time on the beat, I've learned there's no such thing.

Dooling tosses the screen door open and slips inside. He shifts sideways to fit. That's how broad he is.

The giant.

I'm sure he must have expected me to wait on the veranda. Rain on the tin roof masks the sound of my feet as I glide into the house. It is warmer inside than I'd expected. An awkward, sweaty kind of heat, like climbing inside someone else's jacket. The house smells like mice. I make sure to keep an eye on the door.

Playing with fire was one thing. Willingly allowing yourself to be burned alive was another.

I glance down the hall. Hear the shuffling of Dooling's heavy feet. The thud of a cabinet door opening. The rasp of crockery over wood.

Take another step.

There is a staircase on my right. My shoes squelch over the tiles, and I almost slip. I grip the balustrade. The wood is cold.

Hold steady, Detective.

Did Dooling's wife polish the balustrade when she was alive? Was she the house-proud kind? Speculation worms deeper, deeper. Did the ole girl know of her husband's proclivities? Was she aware that beneath the polish there was rot at the heart of her home?

Was this *her* secret?

I see you, I want to tell her. *I see everything.*

Dooling emerges at the end of the hall with a round clay pot in his hands—Pooh Bear with his honey. The gloves have been removed. He bows his head to fit through the kitchen architrave. The light is dim in the hall.

"Didn't know you came in," he says.

I say something about the rain, as if this will do. The cool wind presses against my back. Water trickles beneath my shirt. Icy beads course my skin, down the rise and fall of my spine, down my chest and between my breasts. Tingles. Goosebumps. My flesh is alive. These sensations are a welcoming, and for the first time in a long time—well before AIDS took Matthew, before Amanda Lu came into my office—I *know* I am alive. Every ripple of air between Dooling and I feels predetermined, as if everything was meant to flow this way, this way and no other. I'm meant to be here, on this very day, walking into a monster's lair, led here by things that live when they should be dead. It's April 12, 1991, and if the giant gives me reason to, I'll blow his brains out.

"Yeah," he says. "The rain."

His face is in shadow except for a splash of glow reflecting off a photo on the wall. It lights his eyes. They are bile yellow where they should be white.

My heart skips a beat when something thumps behind a door to my left. Dooling doesn't look in the direction of the sound—an indication I should not look either, that whatever is behind that door does not exist. But it does exist. I know it. And he knows I know it.

Wind whips the screen door. My slicker ripples on my frame.

Dooling smiles, revealing dentures that don't sit right. Horse-like teeth in a sloppy hole. He takes a step into the light, a boot coming down too hard on the tiles. I peek at the sugar pot he holds. Dooling's knuckles are tattooed. The right hand, letter by letter, reads LOVE. And the left would read HATE, had he still his pinkie finger. The stump has been cauterised. No bandages. All scabs.

Another thump from the room on my left.

Followed by a muffled cry for help.

The fake smile on my face remains in place. My hand dives into the pocket of my raincoat and withdraws the gun. I level it at the giant, his lips slinking back over those oversized teeth. "Stop right there," I say. "Back it up. Into the kitchen now."

"What are you doing?"

I lift the gun higher. "Thought you said you lived alone, Dooling."

He scowls. "I didn't say that. I told you I was a widow."

"Who's in there?"

Dooling licks his lips. "Spot," he says. "Such a good boy."

At those words, I fire a warning shot into the ceiling—enough to send Dooling backpedaling down the hallway. The pot strikes the tiles and shatters. Sugar explodes in every direction. Wind catches the grains and sweeps them into the air in a fine mist that catches the light. Dooling dips as he scuttles into the kitchen.

I kick the door on my left. The bones in my body lock and shudder, pieces of me cracking inside. No regrets. The door wasn't locked and swings open.

The words fall out of me. "Sweet Christ, no."

A naked man is on the bedroom floor. He shuffles forward to the extent of the chain about his neck. He's starving. A foot strikes a silver bowl on the ground, raw chicken wings flipping onto carpet covered in newspapers. The chain reaches up to a hook in the ceiling—giving the man enough room to move around but not reach the door or window. Gnarly whippies of shit in the corner. Blood on the walls. His hands are bound behind his back. A gag in his mouth. The colour of the gag is poison mushroom red, the colour of Neville's lips the day he told me I was selfish. The man howls. He rolls, exposing the cut marks across his back and buttocks. Rolls again. Slices to his navel and cock and balls. The man bounds upright again and runs at me, snapping backwards at the taut pull of the chain.

I spin in time to see Dooling re-emerge with a shotgun. My vision flowers with light, my light, my gun. This isn't my first rodeo. I fire a second time. My aim isn't as good as I'd hoped it would be either time. The first bullet missed completely and the second caught Dooling's arm. That is enough. Just. The shotgun falls from his grip as he lands on his side, thrown onto the chequerboard linoleum in the kitchen. I run towards him, Spot keening in his room-cage at my back. Dooling rolls onto his feet with a nimbleness that spits in the face of everything I know about men of his age and size.

Widow power, I think. *Alone power.*

In the time it takes me to get to the kitchen, Dooling has already snatched up a knife. He rushes at me, swinging the cleaver in an arc. I attempt to spin away in time, rewind my steps, heft the gun—only nothing is quick enough. The blade carves the length of my right thigh, through slicker and jeans and flesh. Adrenalin dulls the pain for now. The force behind the giant's attack keeps the knife coursing downwards, inertia dragging the giant to his knees, revealing his bald crown. Opportunity. Knife strikes linoleum. The giant cranes his neck. His eyes meeting mine. I level the gun against his forehead and pull the trigger. The detonation is incredible. Brains sludge across my chest. Bone shards spear my lips and nose. I smell his sick thoughts on me.

Dooling hits the ground so hard the house shakes. He's not quite dead yet. Limbs shudder, his boots squeak-thump the linoleum at my feet as he bleeds out. His mouth opens, closes, opens, closes, the dentures coming unstuck from his gums to clatter in a boney kookaburra laugh in the pit of his throat. I watch Dooling slip away and go still. The moment something dies, it is immediately dead. So dead, so inanimate, it's hard to imagine it ever lived. I've learned this as a cop. But I lived it first as a mother. Something glimmers in Dooling's eyes for a moment, a flicker of light, but then it, too, vanishes. He is cogs now. That and nothing more.

#

I rip the belt off Dooling's blood-stained trousers and fashion a quick torniquet above my thigh. I limp up the hall to Spot, who is rocking on the floor with his head between his knees. I approach him slowly with the gun in one hand and Dooling's cleaver in the other. The boy lashes out in defense.

"Everything's okay," I say. "Let me help you. It's over. He's dead."

I look upon this chained man and see my son on his hospital bed, flanked by nurses who tell him it's okay to let go. And he had a lot to let go of, too. So much anger. Anger at the principal of the school he taught at who fired him once he learned Matthew was gay, worried he'd conscript the kids into the fold. The men and women who called my police department to report when my son went to the local pool where his sarcoma bruises were on display for prying eyes. His father. I choose to believe Matthew let them go, there on his death bed at the end, more tube and machine than man. He gestured at me to come close, his lips parting, wanting to tell me something. But he died before he had the chance. I watched him ease. Saw the monitor turn to lines. Heard that no-pulse whine. Nurses swooped in. A sheet drawn over a face I'd watched change since birth. But the chained man on his knees before me is someone else's son—which isn't to say I'm not proud of him, as I'm sure Scotty would be, too.

Today, this man will live. He has no place on my carousel of the dead.

I rip off the gag. I feel his heat when he puts his brow against my neck and weeps. Scotty told me his friend's name before I left the cabin.

"Are you Proctor?" I say.

He looks up at me. Nods. "He called me Spot."

I cup his bruised cheek and tell him nobody will ever call him that again. "You need to come with me, Proctor."

"D-do you know Scotty?" he asks. "Did he send you? Is he okay? My god, I thought he was hurt. Scotty fought. He bit him. The screams—"

Trying to keep strong, I grip the young man by the chin and make him stare into me. "Scotty doesn't have long, I think. He's at the cabin. There might not be much time. I don't know how this works. I just need you to be stronger than you've ever been. This—" I search for the right words. "This is a goodbye."

It is an awful thing to watch a heart break. I've delivered many death notices over my years on the force, innocent boys and girls carved up or run down or lost. Nothing compared to this honesty. Like so many other things in this world and the next, we must continue to turn. Each and every one of us.

"How are you going to get me out of these chains?" Proctor says.

"The old-fashioned way, honey." I lift my gun. "Cover your ears."

#

Proctor is under one arm. I've dressed him in my raincoat. He's still weighted by his manacles. Tender feet pinch inwards. We cross the stretch of land between the house and the rental, lit by a torch—*the* torch, maybe—I found on a bench in Dooling's kitchen. The hill fights us. The pine forest wants to eat us. But the clouds pull back to reveal stars. They shine bright. The battery in the torch winds down and dies. I'm thankful for the quarter moon that lights the rest of the way.

We emerge from the trees, into the clearing.

Proctor stops us both. He quivers under my hold.

"There," he says, and points.

I lift my gaze to the cabin and see someone standing at the bottom of the stairs. This figure is whole now, and glows with the soft iridescence you sometimes see in a curling wave by night. That glow is elemental. And fleeting.

"Go to him," I tell Proctor. "It's Scotty who saved you. Not me. Not really."

Proctor grabs my shoulder. "Thank you, lady," he whispers.

I nod. It's all I have left to give. Teary, I fight to keep my voice pitched low. "When you're done, I'll take us to the hospital. We're not in good shape, you and I."

"How will you explain what happened?"

I let him slip away from me. My body tingles.

"I honestly don't care," I say. And then I smile. He's not at the smiling stage yet. He may never be. So, I smile for the both of us.

Proctor turns to Scotty, who waits, upright and whole, naked and proud. The light is on inside and the bogong moths launch themselves at the sliding glass door again. I can't blame them. That light is warm.

I watch the two men stumble close to one another. They stop. Proctor lets the yellow slicker grease off his shoulders and pool at his heels. They embrace, flesh to flesh. Cock to cock. Their kiss is deep with history.

It's like the cool valley wind, blowing from behind, wants to usher me closer. I maintain my cop's distance, though there are no suspects here. The gun is still gripped in my bloodied hand. Dry blood. I let the gun go. It makes a soft padding sound against the earth. My shooting days are over. For now, at least.

No promises.

The two men draw apart. Clouds recede further, letting in more moonlight. Voices carry on the breeze.

"Don't go," Proctor says to Scotty. "You can't leave me again. Please."

It is too late.

"Baby, no—"

We both watch Scotty come apart, sliding into pieces like lumps of clay. There is no blood. No pain. This is a return to earth. Proctor cries quietly. He doesn't drop to his knees and try to scoop his lover up. No theatrics. He lets him go. I find this brave.

It's time. I cross the clearing to touch Proctor's neck. "Let's leave this place," I tell him. The pieces of Scotty have become mud at the foot of the stairs. I catch sight of the small starfish shaped earring in the mess. Proctor sees it too and picks it up, rolls it between his thumb and forefinger. "Ha," he says. The memories tied to the earring are his. I do not pry. That life is his. That life has merit. I learned this from my son. Matthew is the teacher. He always was.

Proctor stands, tells me he's ready, and we approach my car parked next to the cabin. I stop. "Oh, I need my keys," I say, leaving him. "They're just inside. Give me a minute."

I step away and approach the cabin for the final time. I have no intention to gather the last of my things inside. They have no value or relevance to whoever I am now. My eyes shift to the door. Through the glass. The keys on the table inside right where I left them.

Bogong moths pound at the door. I grab the handle and slide it open.

"Go on," I say to them. "Now's your chance."

But they do not enter.

ABOUT THE AUTHOR

Author, artist, and filmmaker Aaron Dries was born and raised in New South Wales, Australia. His novels include House of Sighs, The Fallen Boys, A Place for Sinners, and Where the Dead Go to Die, which he co-wrote with Mark Allan Gunnells. His short fiction and illustration work has been published world-wide. Aaron's most recent release is the highly-acclaimed Dirty Heads: A novella of cosmic coming of age horror. Feel free to drop him a line at www.aarondries.com. He won't bite. Much.

ABOUT DEADSET PRESS

Deadset Press is an independent publisher of incredible speculative fiction. We provide publishing pathways for emerging writers from Australia and New Zealand, and aspire to shine the light on unique and diverse voices.

You can learn more at:

www.deadsetpress.com

ALSO BY DEADSET PRESS

Radcliffe by Madeleine D'Este

A three-storey ramshackle house in North Melbourne is full of secrets.

Tamsin is lead to the building by a voice inside her head that tells her

'Death is Coming'.

With no respite from the eternal summer heat, can Tamsin find out who death is

coming for and solve the riddle of Radcliffe?

Sage is searching for her lost brother - the only other family member to survive when the dragons attacked their village ten years ago - and will do whatever it takes to see them reunited.

However a chance encounter with an injured dragon changes her destiny. Against her will, Sage is bonded with the dragon Sahva and becomes an outcast from human society. When she realises that not everything she's been told about the decade-long war is true, she must decide if she trusts Sahva enough to work with him to end the bloodshed.